To everyone who has ever been homeless, or young, or both, or wondered how we ever lived without mobile phones.

CONTENTS

Chapter 1 .... *1*

Chapter 2 .... *8*

Chapter 3 .... *15*

Chapter 4 .... *26*

Chapter 5 .... *39*

Chapter 6 .... *47*

Chapter 7 .... *59*

Chapter 8 .... *66*

Chapter 9 .... *84*

Chapter 10 .... *94*

Chapter 11 .... *100*

Chapter 12 .... *122*

Chapter 13 .... *133*

Chapter 14 .... *157*

Chapter 15 .... *175*

Chapter 16 .... *192*

Chapter 17 .... *209*

Chapter 18 .... *219*

Chapter 19 .... *233*

Afterword *250*

'Daisies bloom where they find room,
This is true of people too.'
- Anon.
(Greetings card: 1980s)

Chapter 1

It was definitely a deliberate fondle - and with all five digits too. Another lurch and Carol edged a further centimetre into the large lady's cold, soft upper arm. Her own left arm was sending out small silent warnings that she was at the end of her tether. Her right arm was jammed between a shoulder and her own right breast and was threatening to go into cramp at any second, while somebody's umbrella was digging into her upper thigh.

She was cornered.

She was looking down into the brown eyes of a small child who gazed up complacently from a shelter of posteriors, pin-striped and navy-crimplened, which hovered benevolently around her head. Carol was looking down at her over a canyon-wall of adult bodies. Theirs was the only eye contact. Everywhere else, heads were averted from averted heads, eyes stared at others' ears or were locked into the most expensive middle-distance in the city which was plastered every inch with promises and rocking slightly as the train hurtled through the darkness.

There it was again - from the canyon wall behind

her had sprouted a frond with five sweaty, grasping petals.

Her behind tried to either shrink or scuttle round to the other side of her but could do neither so was the target of another assault.

Carol jerked her head around as far as it would go to try and see and put a face to the hand. A wall of collars, chins and noses blocked the view but then, one pair of eyes - almost out of her vision - looked straight towards her and smiled.

Hampered as she was, with twisted neck, squashed breast, cramped arm and daggered thigh, she summoned up the most withering, hate-filled glare she had ever inflicted on a fellow mortal.

Before she had to turn back, she was rewarded by seeing his smile widen and relax into a grin, delighted at her anger and her attempt to escape. Carol braced herself again as the train reached its next station stop and then the paw was at her again – bolder than before.

The doors opened. The large lady moved suddenly and Carol fell into the acreage left clear. She tried to find a crowd to hide in - herding for protection. This strategy derives from the principle that if there are enough alternative targets around you, you are less likely to be a target yourself and need only hide in amongst them.

The North American Bison relies on this strategy.

So did the Dodo.

A portion of commuter flooded in to the underground train, flowed around her, threw up a dozen limpets to grasp a hold in this new cave, fixed its eyes into the middle-distance and switched off.

A newspaper-reading commuter was now between Carol and the malevolent Spider - a widely-grinning Spider now, seeing her panic-stricken flight and flustered face. Carol hid behind the newspaper-reader and felt safe enough to park her briefcase by her feet, grab a handrail and concentrate on the mysteries of the Underground Map, trying to calculate whether or not she was lost again. She was running short of time.

Carol could still feel Spider's eyes on her and checked from the corner of her eye that she was still out of grope.

She could not see his leer at first as most of her field of vision was blocked by a glinting, swinging, purple, triangular, plastic honeycomb dangling near the end of her nose from the newspaper-reader's ear. Beyond this earring, and the print-rapt profile, Spider was leering again but not at Carol this time, but at the new target in front of him, vulnerable and unaware, lost in her newspaper. Carol watched him.

He edged a fraction closer to hide what he was going to do. Carol couldn't see his hand but saw his shoulder shift slightly.

The newspaper-reader looked up.

She looked at Carol first and Carol found herself gazing into a heavily mascara dark-brown hell where people lost their lives for less and somebody had better get out of range.

Carol was innocent. A brief burn of surveillance established that - taking in her wide-eyed, horror-struck expression, the ill-fitting suit and the hair slide - then the gates of hell were lost behind a heap of badly-cut, part-dyed dreadlocks which swivelled into their place.

Then the Spider was discovered.

Carol watched his leer twitch into a grin - for just a split second under that dark-brown glare before withering into his chins. Then, from somewhere very near, something like a large, impolite parrot started telling the "pathetic ball of slime" exactly what he was at the top of its lungs - and lots more besides - and every face in the train turned to see.

The newspaper was snatched together into a club and brought down like a flimsy truncheon on Spider in rhythm with the words - loud, lots of them and every one accurate.

Spider scuttled towards the door, arms and shoulders raised against the attack, pushing against the watching wall, searching blindly for a corner to die in. At a station, the doors slid open, the crowd parted and he stumbled out into a row of gaping shoppers on the platform.

" ...and next time I'll be carrying an axe you sad little twerp!" the newspaper reader shouted after him, leaning out of the doors and brandishing her now rather battered paper.

The 'sad little twerp' - once a Powerful Malevolent Spider - disappeared. None of the shoppers on the platform seemed to be mad keen to get on that particular carriage. The silence, before the doors closed and the train moved off, was deafening.

Carol hadn't meant to but she started clapping in applause and a few others joined in. The newspaper reader smiled, bobbed a curtsey, muttered something

4

and sat down. Carol sat down too but the woman with the earring had returned to reading the remnants of her paper before Carol could think of what to say to her.

Carol re-checked the map, re-settled her briefcase, re-clipped her hair slide and started going through likely interview questions and answers again, for the umpteenth time.

Carol stumbled off at the next stop into an army of polite the suited gangsters who surrounded and escorted her to their pre-planned destiny of white-tiled corridors, escalator, ticket-barrier, stairs then abandoned her to a blare of daylight, cars and newspaper-vendors where she escaped their custody and could pay attention to why her arm was feeling so strangely redundant.

The briefcase. Her briefcase. Or rather, Ken's briefcase, which she had been clutching for the past two-hundred miles, wasn't there. It appeared like a risen accuser in her mind: brown and small, kicked and neglected in a carriage full of strangers, abandoned to the mob. Ken's daily companion, his base camp in the wilderness…

…guilt saw its chance and rushed in.

After all his support and care…

She turned to run back, but the backs of a thousand were already heading for the new trains which had pulled in. Ken's treasure-chest of important documents and even more important, salami-and-mustard sandwiches, with the crusts cut off, was lost, flying under all their feet and beyond, escaping under the shops, offices and highways, tunnelling its way out of their lives forever. And, what's more, Main Support Prop in this afternoon's opening performance of Woman About Town, 1983 Cool, Calm & Collected & Well Able to Do the Job and Worth Every Penny of £6,000 pa Before Tax or Thereabouts, pro rata.

With the briefcase, she had looked the part. Without it she looked like she was just another girl from the sticks out shopping.

Carol gaped with uncertainty. What must she do now?

The regular beat of the unintelligible yell from near her left stopped like a heart seizure.

"You alright, darling?' the vendor's voice was harsh with misuse. "You gonna buy one or just look at the pictures?" he went on.

Swimming into view out of the blurred world she had been staring into were a very large pair of carefully air-brushed breasts and, she supposed, never having received one before, an alluring smile.

"Better pictures inside you know," the vendor reassured her, encouragingly.

Carol switched her stare to his used tea-bag of a face as he carried on helpfully, hopeful of a sale, "Good quality too."

"My briefcase," Carol mumbled, by way of explanation.

"You move along now if you don't want to buy anything," he said warily.

Why did all the nutters hang out on his patch? He doubled over coughing, his chest rattling.

His face reminded her that she'd lost her map. She spotted an A-Z and grabbed it.

"You'll 'ave to pay for that," he said, warily, but she handed him the money out of her handbag and headed for a low wall to sit on and work out the next stage of the mystery tour.

"There's no pictures in that!" he called after her but no one heard him or seemed to think it amusing so he returned to yelling out garbled headlines fused with occasional obscenities or personal views on the hurrying, unhearing world.

Chapter 2

"This yours dear? Don't leave it lying there; someone'll think it's another Irish bomb or something. Could you move it for me dear? Let the old girl sit down and give her face a rest. That's better! Thank you dear. Must be my lucky day, they're usually sitting on the roof or running alongside by the time I get here. Comes of working shifts I reckon..."

She continued complaining sociably with the woman across the aisle who nodded and smiled but whose only language might have been Dutch for all she got the chance to say. Anna took the briefcase the woman had handed to her, opened her mouth to protest that it wasn't hers but closed it again in the face of such overwhelming opposition.

It was that girl's. The one who had applauded. Anna took the case and put it on her lap. "Thanks."

'K. Blythe' said the name tag. Kathy? Katy? Kay?

Inside there was a jumper, pale blue and woolly, a flowery toilet bag, some pale and lacey underwear and a plastic sandwich-box - still full.

A cautious person this Kathy/Katy/Kay - Anna's

own supplies for a day's outing were usually all eaten before she got past Earls Court.

There was no cash. Anna was disappointed. But there was an opened letter: it invited a 'Miss Carol Prempton' to interview on the 22nd - that was today, at two o'clock, that was soon, and it gave an address and a telephone number. There was a map showing where 'D.C.L. Ltd' could be found. It was a subsidiary of 'Carmichael and Sons', it said at the bottom of the page. Something echoed but died at the back of Anna's mind then it was her turn to get off, taking the briefcase with her.

She hesitated, suspending it, relieved of the wearable or edible parts of its contents, over an overflowing refuse-bin on the way out of the station.

The sight of Carol came back to her: sat next to her on the train, having applauded her for having a go at that mauler, anxiously reading and rereading the underground map on the wall above her, starting up at every station, worried she had missed her stop.

It was a vulnerable picture.

Anna took the sandwiches and the clothes back out of her own bag and, feeling virtuous, returned them to the case and looked up the phone number on the letter. She left a message with the aloof-sounding receptionist of 'Carmichael & Sons', pushed her way out of the urine–scented phone kiosk and, carrying the two bags, walked down the cul-de-sac of three-storey-houses from the last century, most of which were still officially lived in.

The two houses which were exceptions and which were, officially, empty, peered at each other at the end of the little street, through the luxuriant greenery of their tiny front gardens. Stark oblongs of every shade, from new bright yellow to dead grey-brown, blanked out some of their windows. The pale, once-white plaster, shaded to brown and yellow, gaped and sagged with exhaustion, showing the reddish-brown bricks beneath. The basement windows were buried behind greenery and strange, distorted metal objects, twisted and rusted out of recognition, which lay amongst the weeds like souvenirs of a household war.

The planks and boards across the doors had been ripped away and wary paths trodden through the forbidden wildernesses.

Anna walked up the path to the one to her right where a knot of chain was looped through the hole, that had once held the doorknob, and through a gap, knocked between the door-frame and the old brick of the wall.

Anna unknotted the chain, pulled it through and, out of habit, shoved at the door with her shoulder - and nearly fell inside. Experimenting, surprised, she swung it back and forth. It just brushed the maroon floor tiles where the drag marks of months - or years - had carved quarter moon circles on the floor tiles. The dry-spell must have shrunk it, or maybe they had fixed it before they had left?

She went inside, closing the door. She was standing in a cold-smelling cave, dark - except for a square of light on the landing-wall above which let some grey light filter down over the little half-gate at the top of the second flight. As always, when she came in, she had a sense that things had stopped-happening on her entry - as in a classroom when the teacher returns - and were awaiting her departure to spring into action again, out of the dark.

Here, on the ground floor, chinks of light showed where the boards didn't quite fit over the windows. Rolls of ancient lino and rotten carpets lay in the shadows of the hall. There was debris of ripped out plaster and skirting boards where 'mindless vandals' had visited and probably made a few bob out of the house's boarded up carcass. The copper wiring had been ripped away for the-same-reason and the spaghetti of black, grey and maroon cables which curled about the first-floor were a do-it-yourself Electricity Board Shareholder's nightmare of free light and heat.

Something scuffled in the old lino but Anna made a determined effort not to hear it. Rats sometimes came in under the door to hunt for anything edible which might be lurking in the damp dark - that was the reason for the little half-gate on the first landing they had put up last autumn.

Caroline had told them - tearfully of course - about 'poor little' children dying of rat-bites in their homes in American cities. They had not slept for a week afterwards but then they had fixed up the little gate. Anna locked it behind-her now and carried her own bag, and Kathy/Katy/Kay's briefcase, into the main room.

She had never been in the house alone at night before. Not all night. Even now, in broad daylight, it was strange to think that no-one was home, or would be coming home. Tomorrow she would put the word round and get some more people in. This big room, full of sun and dust, would be drier, probably safer too, she thought, with the two doorways as possible exits. But she pushed that thought away and focused on the fact it would be drier than any of the smaller rooms being the reason she was choosing it.

This place had been her home for nearly a year.

Allan's too. He had left, moving into Caroline's 'pad' – a far more salubrious setting for their wonderful romance. The others must have left too – also moving onto better things, no doubt. Leaving a trail of shapes on the wall where their posters and pictures had been sticky-taped over the cracks.

"And good riddance!" she told the faded rectangles. "It'll be nice to get some peace round here!"

It was strange not to hear a sarcastic reply to this. Not to hear anything at all. She listened to the absolute tension of the silence; the tiny clicks and creaks of the house shifting. It felt like a strange house now the others had gone.

But the last few months, after Allan had gone, had been one, long, harrowing, wrenching then, eventually, boring fight between the other two. Anna hadn't noticed this so much before he had left, being caught up in her own similar rows with him. This left Anna in an unasked - for honorary ringside seat acting, in turn, as buffer, scapegoat, referee, messenger, peace-maker, provocateur and coach. But not tag partner - although that had been requested. Anna had given up and emigrated for a few days having seen, at last that the outcome was inevitable anyway and that all the rest was just hot-air and ego-bashing.

Anyway, it looked as if they had finally taken it all on themselves to sort out their lives and left, probably together, and had cleaned up after themselves, which was nice.

Anna wondered what new things they'd find to talk about once they'd got The Relationship sorted out. It had been the sole talking point for so long - like a monolith built around them both, a third entity enveloping them, preserved entirely on analysis of itself: pickled in bickers. Without 'The Relationship' to relate to each other about it would have ended ages ago - it was just about all they had in common. Not that either of them had liked to be told this. Anna had tried pointing it out but their view on this was that she was 'bitter', 'because of Allan' and 'cynical'. Three was definitely a crowd.

Anna disliked being called names or having to admit to a certain level of bitterness so she'd left them to get on with their battle against cynicism. This went on in multi-decibel mono-syllables for the most part with silent depth-charges of resentment for variety, which could go on for hours until they exploded at the tiniest touch of the push-buttons marked "Ego", which they both kept at red-alert. Then there would be a hearty exchange of personality assassination and rich language.

Anna would try and keep out of this – although she would make notes. You never knew when such knowledge and language would come in handy.

And then, at late afternoon, usually, or early evening, the truce would start and the "making-up", non-verbal, would begin and go on. All night. Or so it would seem to Anna, exiled to the next room and trying to get some sleep.

She had never once been asked to participate in this part of the negotiations - which seemed highly unfair as it seemed, by far, to be the most enjoyable.

But by the following morning she'd be called in again to referee as hostilities would have broken out once more and they'd all go around again. It got quite tiring.

They said they were looking for a compromise. Like the one, Anna thought, that the axe makes with the tree?

Anna unpacked her bag, fetched some water from the rain-butt and put the kettle on for some tea, leaving the problem of the strange violin case and what it was doing there until later.

An opened brown envelope was on the packing-case table. Inside was another eviction order. She put it in the bin.

Anna had asked 'Ms Carol Prempton' to call round tomorrow for the briefcase. She'd have some tea then go over to the other squatted house opposite and see how Liz and the others were getting on. Tomorrow she'd get back on the hunt around for some theatre work. It was 1983 and there was not much about. Her pub jobs would still be there at weekends at least.

Chapter 3

The D.C.L. (Ltd) head-office was down the side of one street - half of which was on the edge of the top of a left-hand page in the A-Z while the other half was on the bottom of a right-hand page at the other end of the book. Carol wished she had brought a compass.

The locals weren't exactly overflowing with enthusiasm when a lost soul asked to be put on the right track. A shrug, a grimace and hurry away seemed standard reaction to requests for help and she considered them all callous, until it occurred to her that maybe they, too, were lost.

Eight wrong turns and an unnecessary bus-ride later she was there.

The main entrance of this subsidiary of Carmichael's was halfway down the street, through a car-park, up a flight of pale-grey steps topped with smoked glass doors and smoking security guards. The rest of the building WAS the rest of the street: a shining wall of metal, glass and concrete, a vast perpendicular chessboard towering up into the grey sky.

Tiny figures could be seen, from the waist up, trapped, here and there, in the mesh; little patches of colour caught in the grey, their faces only distant blurs.

Doesn't look very Limited, thought Carol, awed.

Up the steps, through the glass doors, up to what must be the reception desk, watched by the two guards.

"Miss Prempton," said Carol to the top of the head behind the desk, "I'm here for the interview, I'm a bit late I'm afraid..." She tried not to sound afraid.

"Interview? Who with?"

Carol showed the letter.

"Ayd'ee?" said the hand which had appeared in front of her, pink nail varnish bitten.

"Sorry? What?"

"Your I.D," the receptionist repeated, looking up from her desk. "Identification?" she clarified on sight of Carol's bewildered expression.

Was she old enough to be out on her own?

Carol felt herself flush red, of course, her dad had told her about this, and she dug around in her handbag. Her proffered post-office book and her old bus-pass disappeared behind the desk.

The receptionist checked them, tapped keys on a small machine then turned away to answer a telephone. Carol waited then the machine buzzed and hiccupped and Carol received her 'ID' back, together with a plastic tag with a clip and her name, magically emblazoned upon it. 'Carol Prempton: Visitor'.

"Mr. Pearce's office. Fifteenth floor. Go through," said the receptionist with an attempted jerk of the head, already fully re-occupied with holding a receiver in her chin, saying 'Hmm' into it, watching the notes her hand was making and keeping an eye on the progress made by her teeth on another nail.

"Thank you," said Carol, looking around for something to go through.

All she could see were plastered walls - with windows the only alternative - which seemed a harsh judgment for being a bit late, and St Peter hadn't bitten his nails in any Bible she had ever read. But there was a door, cleverly camouflaged in the up-to-the-minute decor.

Carol marched purposefully towards it and tugged at it efficiently. "Push," said a snotty little note carefully hidden right in front of her nose. She blushed again.

A smart executive type, with an armful of papers went through, ahead of her and held the door open for her, smiling down at her as she walked through.

"Thank you," said Carol.

The door led to a little room especially for the lifts. It was tastefully decorated with plants and pictures.

"Which floor would you like?" smiled the smart executive type, his hand hovering over the rows of buttons as if choosing her a sweet.

"Fifteen," said Carol, and, "thank you," she said, for the third time in less than a minute - beginning to feel like a charity.

A silence followed. The lift had a mirror and its

very own fitted carpet. She noticed the executive type was watching her.

"I'm Tom," he said suddenly, smiling some more. "Do you work here?"

"Not yet. An interview."

"Ah! An interview. A Big Day then!"

Carol smiled, feeling foolish.

They got out at the same floor; Tom helpfully pushed the right office door open for her to go in. It was an office in the backwaters of corridor where there were no carpets, only shiny linoleum and no pot plants.

"A Miss Prempton to see you, Arthur!"

"Thank you Tom," Carol heard from within the office, past Tom's raised arm.

Tom let her pass, whispered, "Good luck," and the door closed on his smile.

Carol found she was being stared at by a large man from behind a small desk. He was standing, looking at Carol and looking flustered and puzzled at the same time.

Carol extended a hand hopefully, aware that it was well lubricated. Her heart was pounding away and her face was flushed.

Generally, her nervous system was helpfully preparing her for an attack on (or from) a sabre-tooth tiger when what the twentieth century required was that she looked cool, sat quietly and came up with the right answers.

But she needn't have worried - the 'tiger's' paw

was also sweaty.

He sat down and his mouth smiled from beneath anxious eyes. He fished out a piece of paper from a heap in a tray and looked at it and then at Carol. She recognised her carefully penned letter and tried to see which were the bits he'd underlined.

"Yes, Miss Prempton, well then, yes, we'd best make a start then… well, you haven't done anything like this er, sort of work before then I see?"

"No," Carol said, cleared her throat, said it again and smiled.

They went on through the letter in much the same way: Arthur leading the way and informing Carol of bits about her life and Carol nodding or saying 'yes' or 'no' to verify his correct interpretation of her literary efforts. They reached the end of the letter. Arthur adjusted his watch.

"Well then, about the job, er, position, you'll be replacing Mrs T. who is expecting a happy event, a great loss, shame she had to go. She was most upset. Still. You'll be working for me, part-time of course but only for a while until we see what comes up when the dust settles. We'll be getting one of those new-fangled wordy-thingies by then for this section of the department, all being well, but I do like to see a human face about the place, at least for a while so, here we are."

Carol nodded and swallowed and tried to look as if she'd never expected a 'happy event' nor ever would, which became too complicated an expression so she gave Arthur a bland smile.

Arthur smiled back benignly then put his hands in

his pockets and leaned back in his chair, looking at the ceiling.

"Now the pay, of course, isn't perhaps as high as some people would like to expect but the experience we feel we offer to a young, up-and-coming office worker goes a long way in today's world as I'm sure you're aware..."

He looked at Carol for confirmation of her awareness. She nodded eagerly.

"And at the end of the year, or whenever, I'm sure you will be more than ready and prepared to move on, as it were, to pastures new with this valuable experience? Hmm?"

Reaction was required here so Carol nodded enthusiastically - trying to look as if she would be ready to move on then, but wasn't now - which was, again, too complicated an expression so she gave another bland smile. Realising he was still looking at the ceiling, she murmured a 'yes'.

He beamed at her again and resumed reading his script off the ceiling.

"You'll want to know what the job, er, position entails of course. Well, mostly typing of course and working between here and the section downstairs. Most of the stuff is kept on computers now, pretty basic and your qualifications cover it, but we do need a lot of ordinary filing sorted out, it's become rather disorganised since Mrs T had to go. This firm, or this part of this department of the firm, deals mostly with Development. It's a very old company..."

He relaxed into automatic pilot and stood up at this point to wander up and down between his chair and the coat stand, hands in pockets, telling Carol the history of the Firm with large chunks of the history of Mr Arthur Pearce thrown in for human interest. The two seemed to have weaved and waltzed their way down the years in a giddy partnership of mutual esteem to the present day.

Carol drifted away into a daydream.

She hadn't been aware that the 'position' was either part-time or temporary. The advert had said nothing about that. No doubt that was why it had only been advertised locally, here in London.

Her sister had seen it in one of the London papers. Still, if she could just get this one - and the competition wasn't much in evidence - it would be a start. She could make the big move to London, live at Dorothy's and then look around for something better. It was a start. That was the main thing. Yes, her qualifications were good, though she hadn't been able to get a place on the best course. Ms Edwards had told her that London was the place for openings - experience was what she needed.

Wasn't that what she had been telling Ken all this time - that she hadn't come this far, sitting Diplomas and evening classes in typing and 'word-thingying', GCSE's and whatnot just to chuck it all in?

Through the window, behind the hypnotic pendulum of Arthur's pacing through the past, lay London: all rooftops and spires, all the theatres and the glamour and Oxford Street and different people and Trafalgar Square... she wanted to see it all. She wanted it all. Small town life was stifling. She wanted out.

She switched back to the immediate present.

Arthur was slowing down, the tone of his voice implying conclusion. Her mind raced to hunt down intelligent questions with which to impress him and make him let her have the job.

"…and so that about completes the picture, Miss, er, Prempton," said Arthur, coming in to land. "Anything else you'd like to know?"

He looked pointedly at his watch.

Carol had quite a few questions left on the prepared list and picked the most important sounding.

Half an hour later, when Arthur opened the door for her and said, "Addeeyur," in a friendly style, the questions had multiplied, but she knew a lot about Mr Arthur Pearce, his wife Clara and their dog, Springer.

The questions she had been advised to ask were 'safe' topics – "Don't ask about wages or they'll think you're a troublemaker," - and had produced voluble and complex replies complete with edifying anecdotes.

She understood her work was to be, "Oh, very general really, you know," and that the people she'd be working for were, "A very nice bunch for the most part," and that her hours would, "Vary quite a bit actually I should think, week to week, keeps you young, nothing like variety, and do you live locally?"

Unable to give a truthful answer, and not remembering exactly where Dorothy lived, nor able to read the upside down address she had put on the letter to make it look as if she was local, Carol had said, "Yes," and he'd said there'd be no problem with flexible hours then, to their mutual relief.

Seeing her to the door, Arthur said 'they' would write and let her know as soon as possible, he told her it had been a pleasure and goodbye.

In the lift again, in the late afternoon, Carol felt vaguely confused. It hadn't been like she had expected at all. Her first real interview - more like a friendly chat! After all the time she'd sat up memorising stuff about computer programming and font-styles and such...

"Ms Prempton?" she handed back her I.D. tag and the tired-looking receptionist stopped her. "There's been a phone-call message for you. Someone found a briefcase belonging to you and will you call for it tomorrow? This is the address."

The briefcase found! Things were really looking up! Carol glowed a smile of a thank you, took the proffered square of paper and wafted out on a cloud of well-being. Plenty of time to get to Dorothy's. She wouldn't bother finding a phone box and phoning home - they knew she would only be going back home straightaway and not staying at Dorothy's if she finished very early. Dorothy didn't have a phone and she'd be half expecting her anyway. Carol decided that she'd have something to eat, right in the middle of London first, and then get to Cambridge Crescent - or was it Gardens? - in time for a good chat with her sister. Maybe she could persuade her to take her out on the town somewhere before going home tomorrow...?

*

At the same time that Carol was leaving the vast building, in a large room on one of the upper floors, far above floor 15, a group of people who were sat around a long table, were raising their hands in a vote. The decision was being made, agreed by most, that, given the currently low levels of interest rates on savings it would be best to move funds out of banks and into various projects which had been 'on hold ' for a while. Some voted against, but it was carried. Lunch was next on the agenda.

The director, Mr Carmichael, left it to one of his new minions, an Adam Singleton, new kid on the block and one of only two black faces in the room, to activate the plans. Carmichael strolled over to the main window and watched the late afternoon sun reflecting on the sea of rooves. A tiny ant–like creature moved across the car park far below him. He looked out over London – boring London.

He was glad this visit would be over soon and he could get back to his home. He had to visit occasionally and check all seemed well for form's sake but he was glad he could leave dreary London and the drearier business of organising the making of huge amounts of money to his lessers. Singleton was alright - for a coloured or whatever you were supposed to call them these days. One had to move with the times, but he did prefer them to be serving the drinks on his local beach.

After the meeting, where the big decisions and overall grand design was agreed, several decisions had to be activated – some large, some small. These then generated even smaller memos into smaller parts of the bigger decisions, affecting smaller lives.

One memo, about one of the very small decisions, was sent to a Mr Arthur Pearce. He had never set foot in one of these meetings or taken part in one. He received the memo the following Monday and then left a message for one of the young architects the firm had recently employed a few times.

The message confirmed that the new project they had spoken about was to go ahead.

Chapter 4

Several suburbs away from where Carol was heading back to the tube station, Allan set down his pint and decided it was time to make a magnanimous gesture. He turned to, or on, his companion.

"So why don't you just jack in this brilliant career of yours, whatever it is and come and live with us for a while? Caroline wouldn't mind. Her flatmate's room's still empty. Place is way too big for us two. I'm on my own in the day while she's at the gallery. And you'd start meeting the right sort for a change, who can appreciate you for what you are. They love artist-types. Didn't do me any harm, Why not?"

"No thanks, Allan. Thanks all the same. It wouldn't work. Don't think it would suit me."

Ralph had lived with Allan before and was in no hurry to repeat the experiment.

"Rubbish. It'd suit you until you didn't know what hit you." Allan was certain. He was always certain. "You've got to push you know. Push, push or you'll get nowhere. Take my word for it. I made the move and look at me."

Ralph looked at him and tried not to wince.

They had once been friends. At school they had been in the same class and then at college the music had been common ground enough and they had shared a house for a while. That they were friends no longer seemed to have completely escaped Allan's notice.

Still, he was buying so Ralph supped the warm beer and listened to the success story again. Allan kept re-telling it - as if he was checking to see what was missing.

"They can help you get on you know," he confided. "No good having talent if no-one sees it."

They wouldn't see it if it shat on them, Ralph confided to the ashtray by way of telepathy. Unless the price tag was big enough to give them a hint.

"I think I'd have to have been dead for a few hundred years to get their notice," he said aloud, "but at the moment I'm a dodgy investment. I've had a few gig sessions - not led to anything but… you never know."

He had met some of the occupants of Allan's new world with Caroline and he hadn't been smitten. They were all looking for something to invest in - pork-bellies, nerve-gas, an unknown musician's career. Being prodded to see if he was a sound commodity had felt odd to Ralph who wasn't used to talking to people that way. They probably found Allan entertaining - which would last for a while, at least, but that would be all, Ralph reckoned.

"You're wrong. A few gigs with bands no-one's heard of? Look at me," Allan demanded again, although he hadn't changed. "Tidy little flat, well, tidy big flat, good address, good contacts, warm bed, warm bed mate who supports me financially – so I've got plenty of time to compose, use of her car, plenty of parties… What have you got?"

Nothing at all crossed Ralph's mind at this point. And that was the right answer. He'd finished the course and not a lot had opened its doors since.

"Has she given it all to you, then?" Ralph asked, genuinely surprised. "I thought she'd just moved you in for some entertainment before the grouse season starts? You be careful and keep up the old contacts. This season's bit of rough - next year's chip paper. It's just a phase is 'Roll-a-prole'. All debutante's go through it. You're probably a great lay and something to frighten daddy with before she toes the line and marries a title. Just in time to turn out a string of heirs. She won't do that with some commoner like you. Don't see how that'll help you and your brilliant career."

"No need for that. Me and Caroline have got a good thing going. A really good thing – so don't knock it…"

"Chickens go home to roost Allan, get real, especially when the coop's so well-lined."

"So you think I'm just a plaything? What's wrong with that? It's a good game, I'll tell you that," Allan grinned into his beer. "She's taught me a few moves, I can tell you…" he began, confidentially.

"I hope you get what you want. That's all," said Ralph, quickly, not wanting to have nightmares later. "Written anything lately? Any actual engagements from all these wonderful people she's introducing you to? At least I'm still out there trying."

"Well no, bit busy, parties, holidays - you know. They're more into paintings and sculptures really."

"Yes, by dead people. Like I said. You see it's not the art - it's just what it's worth on the market - they're the sort who buy van Goghs and then stick 'em in a safe 'til the price goes up. You watch it, they'll do that to you if they think you're a good bet."

"Caroline, actually, is quite the little rebel I'll have you know. No need for that," he added, as Ralph snorted into his beer. "This is true. She's always having rows with that father of hers. It's true! She's a lady of good conscience. You're an inverted snob that's all!"

"She's taken you to meet him?"

"Not yet."

"Who pays for the Porsche?"

"It's hers. It was a birthday present - from her dad."

"Did they row about that?" Ralph decided to humour him as Allan had the decency to look sheepish. "I'm sure she's tearing down the establishment from the inside, like you say. Softly, softly."

"She just has a taste for good living."

"Haven't we all - and so what's she doing with you?"

"People like her just have the means, that's all..."

"Kindly provided by Daddy?"

"But she hardly ever speaks to him! She hates what he does."

"What does he do?"

"God knows, 'sits on boards', whatever that is."

They managed a smile at this one.

"He's a surfer? Cool!"

"He directs things, owns things, makes things and destroys things - I dunno."

"Sounds like Shiva! Has he got a lot of arms? You want to watch your step there mate. Gods can get irate about folk shagging with their daughters."

"She hates him - says he makes money out of doing nothing, other people's work."

"What does she make money doing?"

"Well, nothing - he gives her an allowance out of what he makes."

Allan had to smile again as Ralph pulled a face.

"So she just grits her teeth and takes it?! Must be hell for her." Ralph shook his head in heartfelt sympathy.

"Poor lass!"

"You'd do the same!"

"Wish someone would try me. Is her dad looking to adopt? Tell him I'd take the money and I wouldn't hate him at all. I'd be the perfect son - best smile every day see? Everyone's a winner! Could you ask? We could do a swap. She could be a busker and I could be her dad's kept offspring. Oh no! Wouldn't work."

"Why not?"

"I'd have to sleep with you. Sorry mate, it's the beard."

"Listen, you got on alright with Caroline when you first met her, until you found out who she was - AND you fancied her so you can cut out all this stuff. You're only sore it wasn't you she took a shine to."

Ralph wondered if it was… They'd all met at a college 'do' in support of something or other. Some people had been fighting back somewhere against something – apartheid possibly - and had ended up in prison – funds were needed to get them legal representation. Allan had been the other volunteer soloist.

Ralph had been part of the group who'd organized the gig and had made a bit of a speech afterwards. This good looking woman dressed in designer-anarchist gear had eyed him across the room and then sauntered over to him. She'd looked him up and down and asked if he'd written the final number. More confident than usual, Ralph had bragged a little and talked more about the campaign and asked her about herself. Unfortunately, she had then started wittering on about how it was a 'good cause' but she couldn't condone violence under any circumstances – some people had been arrested for fighting back - and how loathsome it all was and why weren't people reasonable etc. etc. etc. She'd looked at him for some agreement. Ralph had seen the trap. Then he'd proceeded to step right into it.

He could have half-agreed, sidestepped, said she had a good point and stayed in rapport – which he

really wanted to do - and opened his mouth to do it...
Instead he heard a voice, which he recognized as his
own, trying to explain where the real violence came
from and the difference between people with
truncheons, vulcanised rubber outfits and water–
cannon and those in jeans and sandals. His voice
sounded irritated and tired and about as attractive as a
windblown placard.

Small talk had never been Ralph's strongpoint.

Allan, someone he'd been at school with who was
also on the course and who shared a house with
Ralph for old time's sake, had then appeared. He was
dressed to the nines, as he did for these occasions,
looking like a film star and swimming in his natural
element. He caught the tail end of Ralph's diatribe,
saw Caroline's expression and guessed the context (he
had lived with Ralph for a term).

"But there are so many other strategies," he'd
chimed in smoothly, turning to smile into the eyes of
the indignant Caroline, who looked at him and
simpered gratefully.

Their eyes had met.

"Voting, petitions, vigils, letters," Allan had
continued, Caroline nodding, elegantly. Ralph hadn't
thought nodding was something that could be done
elegantly.

"True," Ralph had snarled, no longer aiming for
charm. "All with one thing in common."

"And what's that?" smiled Allan.

"They don't bloody work."

Ralph had done a swift calculation in mental

arithmetic of how long his life expectancy was and how much of it he wanted to spend trying to persuade the Carolines of this world that the poor of the world could only get less poor by the wealthy becoming less rich and that the rich were not going to welcome any such change without a fight and that, despite being wealthy, she really should side with the other lot.

He had then given it up as a bad job, salvaged another glass of wine that was looking lonely and left them to get on with it.

Caroline and Allan had 'hit it off' as the saying goes. They had seemed to spend the rest of the evening discussing the state of the world and how not to change it. Apparently coming to some sort of conclusion, they had left early and together, despite the fact that Allan had come to the 'do' with Anna – a drama student Allan had met some months previously. She'd been in the middle of another discussion elsewhere at the party which could be heard over most of it.

Anna hadn't seen Allan leave and Ralph had feigned ignorance when she'd asked. He felt bad doing that as Anna seemed alright the few times he'd met her but he knew not to get involved between couples. Apart from which, he was behind with his share of the rent again and Allan wouldn't take kindly to him 'ratting 'on him.

Allan had not been the same since. Or more exactly, the less obnoxious characteristics of his besieged personality seemed to have withered in his new environment, while his charmless, self-satisfied arrogance had found its true element and flourished, choking everything in its path and blocking out the light.

It had been sad to watch. It still was.

Allan sipped his beer and carried on with his magnanimous gesture.

"You're still not coming on Saturday, then? There'll be quite a few people there who'd like to meet you. Give 'em a few tunes – they'd go mad for you."

"No thanks mate. I'm busy."

"You're making a mistake, if you don't mind me saying so, it's a good opportunity."

To do what? Stop being a fool and start being an arsehole? But out loud he said, "Thanks, but I'll best stick to what I'm good at."

"We wrote some good stuff – why don't we get together some time and see if we can't come up with some new stuff? Are you working on anything at the moment?"

"Nah! Flat out of ideas." Ralph lied. He suddenly guessed at the reason why Allan had got in touch for this afternoon beer - he'd gone to all the trouble of calling at the squat and leaving a note for him. Ralph had thought, just for a moment, that it was a straightforward gesture of friendship. He might have known better. He always had been naïve. Allan didn't waste time with people he couldn't use and Allan was stuck. Caroline had been impressed with his musical talent. She could show him off to her trendy friends. But the canary had run out of songs. Without them, he was just another better-looking-than-average Bit of Rough.

"You'll have to make the right moves sometime. It's not me who's sleeping in some grubby dump – it's a squat isn't it – the one Anna used to live at? I lived there with her for a while. I've done my time! And living on the dole? You can't do that forever. I'm looking to the future."

"I would if I were you; 'Roll-a-prole' might not be the in-thing next season. Just make sure you're saving something out of that pocket money she gives you. I'm not being funny, this is sound advice..." but Allan didn't look as if he wanted any advice - especially from someone whom he was trying to patronize.

"You're old fashioned Ralph, move with the times. The sky's the limit. Survival of the fittest. Anyone can get anywhere. Look at the PM – she was a commoner. She got ahead."

"By shagging a millionaire? Is that the career advice for all of us then? They could make a Youth Opportunity Scheme out of it to show us how!"

Allan's jaw looked suddenly taut. *How many beers has he had?* thought Ralph. He had embraced this new philosophy. The 'free market', the Great Individual. He probably saw himself in a cape. A hero of the free society.

Ralph backed off. Allan was built like a JCB with sweaty bits after all.

"Sorry mate, I guess I'm just jealous."

Allan relaxed at that and smiled - magnanimous once more. He enjoyed jealousy, especially other people's. It made him feel secure. Or at least it helped.

"I can understand that," he said. "Silken sheets, you know I'm ruined. Have you ever tried it on coke?"

Ralph had to admit that he hadn't.

In fact, he hadn't tried it on anything just lately but kept that to himself.

Allan reminisced into his pint for a while.

"Don't worry Ralph, you'll see the light soon and fix up with something. But you should come around more often and get that chip off your shoulder. Believe me. We had some good times you and me."

"Maybe you're right."

"Seen Anna lately?" Allan changed the subject.

"No, she was gone when I got there who were always rowing. Don't know where. There's no-one else there now. For a while anyway. Thanks for telling me the address."

"Yeah, it was all quiet when I dropped the note round. Still a dump, mind. Anna was alright – but I've moved on to better things!"

He wasn't going to start in on her again was he?

"Bit of alright she was," carried on Allan, "but a bit rough for my liking now - I like a real woman now, Anna was too full of herself..."

"I've got to go soon. Do you want another pint?" interrupted Ralph.

Allan looked at his watch. He took his time doing it, hoping to attract Ralph's attention to the exclusive design but Ralph was looking determinedly in the other direction.

"No, I'd better be getting back I suppose. I'll give you a lift back? Won't take a sec?" Allan was being magnanimous again.

"No ta, I'm calling on someone near here."

"Oh aye, glad to hear it - not that Angie?"

"No, not Angie," Ralph said, looking into the middle distance, his mouth suddenly taut.

"Alright, be secretive," Allan laughed, "but give us a ring, yeah? It's good to get out... visit my roots occasionally... slum it for a change..."

He laughed and looked to see if Ralph was jealous again of his high life and newly-acquired other world. Ralph only felt a sharp need for the door and a lack of Allan's presence so he laughed with him, knowing he'd be gone all the quicker because of the low, muscle-shaped car they had stopped by which was obviously on loan from Caroline.

"See you then, mate," Allan took his time opening the car door so Ralph could get a good look. "Let me know if you reconsider."

He winked and then crawled, doubled-up into the muscle.

Ralph turned down a side-street into the orange pallor of the street-lights and the spitting rain. He turned up his collar and heard the engine roar to impress the locals as Allan drove off, back to his well-lined haven and 'real woman' with the silk sheets and golden dividends.

What a prat.

There wasn't any 'someone near here', of course, just a walk back to the squat in the rain. He'd save the tube fare as it wasn't too bad out but, more importantly, he needed to walk off the tight knot of aggro which Allan had tied in his guts, walk it out into the pavement. Not just Allan but the world he represented which was coming in at him from all sides lately.

Was it anger? Or was it plain envy of an easy, comfortable life-style in a warm flat with the kind of money that made life safe and the world kind with no stupid worries like how to keep sane and healthy for another week and a beautiful woman to share it with and crowds of easy, laughing confident friends around you.

The spitting turned to rain and found a way down his back like slivers of ice. This shirt would take ages to dry unless it was sunny tomorrow. He was out of washing powder again, of course. Lunchtime shift tomorrow - pulling pints. Evening's busking if the rain kept off.

Was he jealous of Allan?

Or had he gone completely insane?

Ralph decided to toss a coin to decide that one. The coin told him he was completely insane which was an enormous relief.

He walked on.

Chapter 5

"I'm sorry, no. No Dorothy here, no people of that name. Have you got the number right? Maybe it's further down - John?"

'John' put down his newspaper and came to the door to look at Carol.

"This young lady is looking for a Dorothy Sell and her husband. Do you know any people along here by that name?"

"Sell? No, I can't say I do," John rustled the coins in his pockets and frowned down at Carol as if she were a cryptic clue and looked beyond her at the trees and bushes along the drive. "But I don't know any of the people along here at all. Where have you come from?"

Carol told him and he sort of hummed and went back inside the porch. His wife turned to him and they hummed and muttered together on the case then he went back inside.

She turned back to Carol and smiled brightly, "I'm so sorry we can't help you. I would invite you in but we've had a lot of burglaries around here lately so we can't be too careful, you understand. That's why we got the dogs. Dobermans you know," she added conversationally.

Carol nodded. She knew. She wondered if she looked like a housebreaker. She didn't know what to do now.

"Well, goodnight then. Frightfully sorry we can't help. Do call back if there's something you want to ask. We'll be in all night. Goodnight now dear."

Carol turned away and went back down the neatly bordered driveway. She didn't hear the door close completely until she'd reached the road again. She looked back at the house. Dorothy would have loved a house like that. But she should have guessed that it was not hers. Then she noticed a gap appear in the curtains and hurried away.

It was not Cambridge Crescent either anyway. And a long walk back to the station and a long ride back into the centre.

Never mind, it must have been Cambridge Hill after all.

She couldn't afford much more of this. Her snack in the middle of London, her treat after the interview, had cost a lot more than she had expected and she had been travelling ever since. Everything in this city cost so much and the fares were fast gobbling up what she had left.

The bright blue and yellow train swept in and roared her back to the Centre. There was the quiet lull of evening in the suburbs but the centre was full of people looking for frenzy. Seeing them, Carol realised how tired and drab she felt. She had been travelling all day since an early start from home that morning.

Maybe she should have caught the train straight home after all? She would have been home by now. Sitting around the telly, looking forward to supper instead of feeling hungry, and telling them all about her day in the City and maybe phoning Ken and going around to see him; he'd be in the pub with his mates now.

She could phone now and ask them to tell her Dorothy's address but how would that look? She'd have to tell them of losing the briefcase and forgetting the address. Much better to say she'd gone to a show and got to Dorothy's late. If she was going to convince them she could cope in the city and be independent she could hardly start out by telling them all that.

At the next station in the centre, another train full of strangers pulled in, staring straight through her from behind the smeared glass. Only a tired trickle got onto this one to replace the sparkling river that flowed out of it into the night's razzle.

At least this ride out from the centre was not so long. But it was another stranger who appeared at the door in the long terrace and Carol almost moaned out loud in disappointment. Home-smells wafted out from behind the woman who all too obviously wasn't Dorothy. Carol felt sick - even if she wouldn't have wanted Dorothy to be living here in a street like this where the 'Park' wasn't much in evidence.

"Yes dear?" the woman prompted when she felt she had waited long enough. The girl looked ill but seemed well enough off with a nice suit and everything.

Carol asked the same question. She was looking for her sister but didn't have the address. The woman listened sympathetically.

"Oh dear," *a feuding family obviously*, "perhaps you'd better come in. We've not been here long, mind, maybe the people who were here before are what you want, I'll get their address..."

"No, no, that's not..." But how could she explain without looking a complete idiot? "I know where I've gone wrong. Really. Thank you."

The woman had turned to go and look for the irrelevant address and looked at Carol again in some confusion. What was the matter with the child?

"I've got the wrong road," Carol floundered, "it must be the other one."

One! She pushed the image of the long list of unexplored Cambridge Terraces, Streets, Avenues and Roads to the back of her mind to save off total panic. She couldn't phone home to check - that would just be proof that she couldn't cope. Then she remembered. Of course! Court! It was Cambridge Court! Of course! How could she have forgotten?

"Goodnight then dear," said the woman. Suspicion had crept into her eyes and she peered more closely at Carol. The door, very slowly and politely, began to close.

Carol turned away from the yellow-lit doorway and the warmth into the spitting rain. She was lightheaded with relief. She would just go straight to Cambridge Court and this would all be a huge joke to share with Dorothy. She looked it up in the A-Z and planned the underground route she needed to take. Fortunately it was not a long one.

The woman watched her go, up the road, under the occasional dull street-light and into the night. She closed the door.

The night was full now - deep and navy. The spitting turned to rain as she reached the station again. She was alone in the compartment this time, except for a someone in a black suit with psychedelic hair and mirror glasses. Its own personal power-pack was strapped to its skull, an alien antennae or proboscis licking at the brains. The head nodded slowly to a rhythm she could barely hear and she could see two tiny miniatures of herself reflected in the creature's eyes. She wished she had a similar pair so they could have sat and looked into endless tunnels of themselves forever and she wouldn't have had to wonder if it was staring at her or not.

Out of the station, there were some cars out on the main road but her way lay down a side-street where the lights were economically spaced and no cars came. The houses crowded the pavement, curtains were drawn and she could hear no sound of life behind them, if there was any to be heard, except for a pattern of insistent voices and music, repeated at every window and an identical square of flickering colours on the back of each set of drawn curtains.

The inmates of every house seemed to be having the same conversation to the same background of violins.

The next turning was lined with small shops, shut up for the night – metal shutters drawn and padlocked. Old newspapers littered the pavement, plastered down with rain and pale yellow in the dull light.

The third turning on the right, the map said.

She heard them very faintly in the distance first. She couldn't be sure how many there were. Or if they were all male. They were definitely ahead of her if she carried on.

Then she heard loud laughter and a crash. She was aware that her breathing had quickened. She could dodge back to the next turning - but they might go that way too. They came into sight: five or six of them strung in a line across the pavement and talking. Loudly. Looking for trouble. Perhaps they were out mugging!

She tightened her grip on her handbag. She could plead with them, tell them that she had no money and had to get home - which was true - but they'd probably laugh at her, maybe beat her up... Oh my God, they were probably rapists, you read about people like this, packs of rampaging animals in areas like this, roving the streets looking for victims. She'd come to a standstill, her heart racing. She couldn't run in these stupid interview shoes and there was nowhere to run to.

She could see their vicious faces now and they had spotted her. They were staring at her and coming closer in silence. She gripped her bag, hunched her shoulders and stared at the pavement then closed her eyes against the black-and-white headlines flashing in front of her: Girl Found: Gangs Claim New Victim...

"Eh, you alright love?"

She stared up into the fleshy face with its puzzled, slightly anxious expression. They'd almost gone past when he'd stopped by the strangely twisted figure in the rain. The others stood a little further on, warily curious. What nut was Stephen talking to now?

The 'nut' stared up at them and hugged something to her. They couldn't see what it was - a baby? A dead cat?

"Come on, Steve, we're late already," one of them said, a little nervously.

"You alright?" he said again.

"Yes, of course I'm alright!" Carol snapped at him.

"Well okay, sorry, you just looked... never mind. G'night," and he hurried away. The others went with him, glancing back at her. She heard their voices after they had turned the corner.

They probably loved scaring innocent people like that, walking about in a big gang and laughing all over the place. She would have showed them. She hadn't been ready but she'd show them. Next time it would have to be.

She'd imagined similar scenes many- times - how she would stare them out; freeze them into shame with her arrogant coolness and self-possession. Icy sarcasm was the secret. She thought of well-turned barbs she could have used – and would use, next time. Walking on, towards Dorothy's, she tried them out on the night air on imaginary and suitably cowed assailants. Next time they could look out. She'd be ready for them next time. She reached the turning. And stopped.

The name of the road was correct but the panic started to rise.

Suddenly she noticed how cold the night was. There was nowhere to go. She was out of money. She was completely alone.

The warm rush of sudden panic left her and cold Fear took its place. The pavement continued past the road-sign for about ten yards. There were no street-lights at all. The house on each corner was the first and last of its row.

Beyond was blackness, stretching away. Lights, as small as stars, crowded in curved patterns in the distance, but here was nothing. Dim meaningless shapes lay in the foreground of the dark - piles of bricks, perhaps, with what could be nettles growing in them.

This was Cambridge Court.

*

Meanwhile, somewhere in the ether, in a different part of the world which was still in daylight, it had been noticed that the worldwide tendency for companies to remove savings and use them instead for investment in production again - due to the lower interest rates - began to mean that the vast stocks of money which had been laid up for quite a while had dwindled. Meetings were held, decisions made. One of these was to raise the interest rates and so slow down the tendency.

Chapter 6

Must be about 2am by now. Must have left the chain back at Liz's. Never mind. Lean this case against the door. Oops. Bit pissed. Not many people about now anyhow. Up the stairs. Drank and smoked a bit much. Nice of Liz to offer a place with them. Until more people moved in anyway. But she could be a bit much. As well as all the others who had moved across to the warmer house leaving this one empty. And a time alone wouldn't do her any harm. A bit of a challenge really. Like getting up these stairs.

No, don't put any music on. Get used to the house's little noises. Silly little noises. Sleep in the big room though. Don't go through to the back. Nasty little room. Like a trap. No, ignore that thought. It was just a nasty little room.

That was all. Take off jacket. Sleep in clothes tonight. Get into warm, soft... no, bloody cold sleeping bag. Mattress on floor. Go to sleep.

No dammit, toilet. Out of warmed-up sleeping bag. Down cold, dark passage. Stop looking over your shoulder. Small, electric-blue room. Freezing cold seat. Forgotten bucket to flush with. Do it tomorrow. Back

down horrible dark passage. Who the Hell's that? Oh –
stupid poster. That's coming down tomorrow. Back
into freshly re-frozen sleeping bag. Sleep.

Uh-oh. Like that was it? No. Sleep! Waste of
energy. Allan not here anymore anyway.

And what did that have to do with it? Some things
he had never got the hang of anyway. No way for an
independent woman to think either. Better than
aerobics as well. Right then, let's see... Allan no
suitable fantasy. Too much recent damage there. Bit
too mainstream anyway. Have to be more imaginative
than that. Or plagiarise? Life wasn't long enough to
turn all fantasies into memories, after all. That had
been one that had appealed. In that book. In a lift.
With whatever his name was. And his friend.
Boyfriend actually. Yes. Slowly though. At first.
Together. And the other way. People looking in
through the window in the door. Taking it in turns
now. Lift rising. People knocking at the door. Who's
this? Whose is this? How did he get in? She actually.
Hm... Complicated. Nice. Up against the door.
People wanting to get in. Trying to get the doors
open. Up against the door. Hands, mouths
everywhere. Stranger's too. Fifth floor. Sixth. Time
running out. All at it now. All different. On the floor.
And watching the others. How did they do that? And
again. Deeper... people watching... wanting to get in...
tenth... eleventh... faces blurring... mouths... doors
going to open not yet, not yet, long. Slow and a row
of faces watching... doors open!

Well, that was a weird one. A shrink could earn a
good lunch out of that one. Weird. Worked though.
All relaxed. Sleep now.

Mind you, it wasn't all that weird. Not when you think about it.

Don't think about it then. Go to sleep.

Wasn't as weird as what's considered normal.

Trying to fit a single mould of the perfect partner forever. Tightrope walk between whore, Madonna and friend and all hell and moral outrage when the thin cord snapped. That seemed to be the norm. With not a shrink in sight and no way out.

Plenty of Valium though. Cheaper. And no wonder... Trying to be other people's fantasies and needing them to be yours.

Tough one that. Reducing yourself to a fantasy's fantasy - and love to a hall of mirrors - all reflections and images, looking each other up and down. But never straight in the eye as that can only happen between equals and even fantasies get put in hierarchies.

Wonder how Allan was getting on with the gorgeous Caroline and her gorgeous apartment? And her gorgeous Daddy and his gorgeous wallet? Poor old thing.

But of course, it hadn't been the money you had wanted. Nor the winters in the sun, the well-kept hair, the exquisite clothes, silken skin, nor the smooth confidence.

Didn't choke on it either, though, did you, my sweet?

Nice person? Yes, I remember the donation she'd made - written out with a slim be-jewelled pen in her slim be-jewelled hand and more than we had collected for the strike-fund all bloody week, standing in the precinct in the rain, hair plastered to raw cheeks, eyes screwed against the wind. Very captivating. And along she comes in her handmade raincoat with her handmade features and her handmade wealth.

Well-manicured hands to have made so much.

Not that she had supported it of course, oh no! But she did want to help. "Those poor dear children."

"What the hell do you think they're fighting for?" I'd asked. "Whose children are they?"

But you had told me not to be so touchy. God knows where you had met her but you obviously knew each other well.

But you'd talked to her. And she'd listened. Oh boy, how she'd listened! All sad eyes and sentiment as you told her about the hardship suffered.

As long as they didn't fight back, it seemed, she could sympathise. A pity people were so unreasonable as to fight back, not come, pitiable, begging for her to play the ministering angel, with her cheque book.

Why is Anger so un-picturesque? Poverty, from a distance, can be retouched in water colours and used to decorate biscuit tins but somehow anger never could.

So you hadn't shown up for the next day's effort and it was snowing and people weren't giving and I got home to a shitty little note from you about some bloody party at her "pad" (Pad! For god's sake!) and I was invited.

Oh joy!

Caught it in the neck that night didn't you, my

love? No, we are not an 'exclusive couple' but the common courtesy of letting me know would have been nice.

So there you are... mopping her socially conscious fevered brow. With fivers. And you're saving her old man some shrink-bills and letting her experience some rough-trade into the bargain - which all helps to make for a balanced, healthy lifestyle. That class needs new DNA every few years after all. But games get tiresome and boring so she'll get tired of her new toy and move on, so make the most of it, my sweet.

The rain started up again and rattled on the windows. Anna decided she definitely would try to get more people in the next day and went to sleep.

*

The first sound must have been very small. Just an echo of it wandered into his mind and reached a few neurons among the millions, nudged them a little and died without making much of an impact. The rest of the myriad were too busy entertaining themselves with complicated unlikely-coloured shapes and faces he barely knew doing weird and wonderful things to each other in strange sequences as the images tumbled by on a wild post-Freudian holiday.

The loud bang and the wrenching crash had more of an effect.

He sprang awake.

The crash seemed to have come from below and to his left but there was a rustling sound, very faint, coming through the door to his right from the other, bigger room. He was surrounded. He lay very still and tried to hold his breath to listen, while his mind, just

51

dragging itself out of a morass of gigantic poppies and twisting skyscrapers tried to come up with an idea of what the hell he was going to do.

*

In the next room, Anna's hand curled very slowly around the neck of the bottle and lifted it by the inch out of its plastic carrier bag as quietly as possible. No further sound had come from below.

She eased herself out of the sleeping bag and, crouching to keep her silhouette below the window ledge, she crept over to the door.

Her heart was gulping adrenalin like an addict but there was nowhere to run and its hammering only deafened her. A stair creaked, someone sniffed, probably drunk or with drug-rotted sinuses. She got behind the door and squatted down to make a smaller target, the bottle held ready.

She glanced back towards her bed - and her heart almost stopped.

The silhouette of a head and shoulders loomed against the night sky in the window.

How the hell had he got past her?

She opened her mouth to breathe more quietly. Then the figure, as she had done, dropped down out of sight into the pool of the dark. She stared into it but could see nothing. Was he creeping towards her? Hands outstretched to grip?

She clutched the cold, smooth bottle more tightly. Should she break it and use it as a knife, or keep it as a club? What could she break it on? The element of surprise was on her side. The green-belt in karate -

why had she stopped going to classes? - would also come in handy. She waited, her heart pounding.

*

Crouching, he moved over to where he remembered the door should be. Very slowly. No noise. Trying not to shiver in the chill air. Then, with a shock, he saw the intruder. He could make him out, very dimly in the gloom, dark skinned, over by the door, crouching and vicious and clutching something. Waiting, with mad, spiky hair and staring eyes and looking towards the window.

He could rush and surprise him, stop him getting out any knife he might be carrying - he might be a pusher, just back from selling white powdered-poisoned-hope to school children at a discount... hooking the homeless and desperate... homeless and desperate himself... prepared to kill as a matter of course.

Probably carried a knife.

Perhaps two or three for different purposes.

Ralph wished he had put more clothes on. He shivered and tightened his stomach muscles, such as they were, against the thrust of the blade.

One rush, grab his arms and hit him as hard as he could...

Oh my God! There were two of them... He couldn't fight two of them!

*

The second figure loomed up outside the door, hovered for a while, then seemed to make up its mind to come in. It lurched forward, one arm outstretched, groping. Anna, on the dark, outer edges of fear, sprang up and desperately swung the bottle high... but before she could bring it down, a huge second figure hurtled out of the dark, pinned her arm against the wall and hit her in the stomach. A horrible scream - not her own - deafened her.

Anna jerked her knee up as hard and as far as she could, he countered with his free arm which she grabbed and got her leg behind his to throw him, he shifted his weight to counter this and grabbed for her neck so she rammed her fist into his stomach. Then the light went on.

"Ralph!"

"Anna!"

"What the fuck you doing?"

"Me?"

They released the various bits of each other they'd been about to assault and straightened up, breathing hard, examining bruised places for signs of blood.

Both were quaking as muscles, tightened to action, suddenly got the message to relax and be sociable.

"So what the hell are you doing creeping about in my place in the middle of the night scaring me half to death?"

"Your place? Since when... you're the one creeping about... I'd got you with this bottle if you hadn't put the light on. And I still might."

"Well thanks! And... I didn't put the light on..."

They both turned to fend off the third attacker... but a figure less like a murdering maniac would be hard to find.

Carol was still holding onto the makeshift light switch she'd grabbed accidentally in the dark and stood, terrified and exhausted. Tears had left their tracks down her face, her hair-slide was lost on a dark pavement somewhere and her eyes knew them for the maniacs they were who had lured her to their den where people fought like dogs in the night as the final episode in her waking nightmare.

"Oh, hello. Kathy? Or is it Kate? Off the train?" Anna remembered.

"It's Carol," Carol's voice was tiny. She recognised the weird black girl who had driven Spiderman off the train and who had left this address for her. "I've come to get my case. I didn't know where else to go. I got your note." She held out the note the receptionist had given to her. An A-Z was in her other hand.

"That's right. Um, wasn't expecting you. Just yet. Come in." Anna straightened her nightshirt and picked up a cardigan to put on. She felt quite dizzy. "Like some tea?"

Ralph didn't quite grasp the situation but tea sounded reassuring so he went to make some. Everyone else seemed to know what was going on. When he got back, the stranger woman of the two was looking through a pink address book.

"Yes!" she said suddenly. "Walk! Cambridge Walk! That's why I kept thinking of trees!"

Ralph decided he would be safer in the kitchen and went back to look for the sugar.

"I got lost," Carol confessed to Anna, who was

standing, shivering, watching her.

It wasn't surprising news.

"I guessed," said Anna. "I think you'd better stay here now."

She didn't ask any questions of Carol: a stranger in London, a lost address and the night - she could guess at the rest from her face and eyes. Good job she had got here. She wasn't dressed for a "night out"- in the fullest sense of the word.

Ralph brought in the tea in two mugs and a glass.

"I thought you'd left, actually Anna."

"I haven't."

"There was nobody here when I moved in."

"I was having a holiday, when are you moving out?"

"You still don't like me do you?"

"Was it you who filed the bottom of the door off?"

"I'll file it back on if it would make things any easier?"

"Do you two live here then?" asked Carol, in between sips of tea. The two looked at each other. Neither was too pleased at the idea.

"Well I've been here for months. How long you been here, Ralph?"

"I've spent all my life getting here. Does that count?"

Anna wasn't impressed. "What happened to the place you and Allan used to share?"

"That job ended, I got behind with things... you know, the usual story. We won't be here long anyway, the number of people they've got snooping around the place. Any day now I should think they'll want us out. Couldn't you stand it for a while?"

"Is this a squat then?" asked Carol, she had heard of such things. "That's against the law, isn't it?"

She was wary of these people.

"So is sleeping on the streets or loitering about wide awake - take your pick," said Anna to Carol. To Ralph she said, "You would have to be on your best behaviour though, I don't want to get attacked every time I come home, I thought you'd come to kidnap me."

"Who'd pay? I thought you were the C.I.D. After me for my life of crime and violence..."

"Why, they having a recruitment drive? You must have been here when I came in?"

"I must have been flat out. Been out with Allan for a drink."

"That must have been a treat. How is the little shit?"

"No bigger. More tea? Oh dear..."

Carol, worn out or just overwhelmed with relief at having escaped the twisting streets and moving shadows was crying, very quietly.

"I'm sorry," she sniffed.

"S'alright, we've all been there. You go right ahead and cry."

Carol did. Then blew her nose and felt better.

They sorted out three quilts, or things like quilts, and settled for the night. They decided to leave the hall light on.

Carol lay awake for hours listening to the noises of her strange refuge. She would get home tomorrow and tell them she'd been to see a film and stayed at a B&B. That would impress them. She'd see Dorothy another time.

She didn't want the family to think she couldn't cope on her own. They'd never let her leave if they knew about tonight.

Images of the night's experience kept revisiting her and she didn't get to sleep for quite a while.

Chapter 7

Angie got on with her drawing and decided Tom was best left alone when he was like this. He sat with his drink, his executive jacket off, and glowered at the television.

"Silly bitch," he said to one particularly vacuous housewife thrown into ecstasy over some carpet cleaner, another one came on, in paroxysms of anxiety over her hair colour.

He glanced over at Angie but she was putting the finishing touches to a design and didn't seem to have taken any notice. He took another swallow of scotch. The adverts ended.

A film came on about aliens.

Tom irritably switched channels.

"They must think we're all bloody morons!"

He switched from a familiar cheery theme tune to a panel of male, pale and miserable faces discussing something. From them, to a passionate embrace between a man and a woman, which progressed during his few seconds of voyeurism, from where the woman beat punily on the unassailable silk-clad shoulders and struggled to escape the attentions the hero was forcing upon her (from the waist up only as this was a family film). This changed to where she was more passionate than he and ran her fingers through his hair - pressed against him (from the waist up only as this was a family film).

"Silly bitch!" Tom muttered and switched over again.

"Hey! I wanted to watch that," Angie looked up.

"I thought you were 'working'. Too-busy to talk to me anyhow."

"I'm sorry but I've got to get this done or it won't go in – it won't take long. I didn't know you were coming round tonight or..."

"Alright, alright, just let me know when you've finished - if I'm still here. I've got a stinking headache."

"There's some aspirin in the cabinet - I'll get you one." She got up, went to the cabinet and fetched him the white tablets and a glass of water, handed them to him but then sat down again with her pen.

Right bloody night this was turning out to be. After a pig of a day with his contract suddenly hung in the balance over some tramps or whatever they were called these days. All his mates he'd expected to see in the wine-bar for a comforting few were all 'otherwise engaged'. Getting some in - that probably meant. And Angie was no good. What would she know about wheeling and dealing and meeting the right names and pushing, waiting and pushing again until the door opened - just a crack, a splinter, not even that. Then it just might be slammed again once more, and maybe forever, over some bloody, spineless, lice-infested nothings who just set up house wherever they felt like it and screwed up other people's lives.

He clicked the television back on, then went over to the stereo, ran the tuner back and forth across the wavelengths and played with the volume switch. He swallowed his drink and got a refill.

There was nothing else about, not on the immediate horizon anyway - not that he'd heard about. He wondered about Arthur sometimes and whether he was really the comfortable old shoe he seemed to be and whether he was keeping any new projects out of his, Tom's, way.

But no, there just wasn't much happening at the moment. Nothing Arthur, or anyone, could do about that. The market had been just more or less dead for a while.

This was the first real chance he'd had since graduating and setting up his architect business on borrowed money – part of 'the new enterprise economy' - and now it looked as if even this might be snatched away.

He poured another whisky from Angie's cocktail collection, put on a record and got the new headphones on. Angie looked up briefly and smiled at him. If the worst came to the worst he could always change the car for something cheaper to tide him over. Maybe take in a lodger – he hated the thought of that. Angie was forever dropping hints about them moving in together. Maybe a lodger wasn't such a bad idea. He could borrow some more of his dad – but he hated that idea too. He could envisage the disapproving look and the heavy sigh as he'd reach for his chequebook. He was getting on for 30 for Chris-sake. Wasn't he supposed to be successful by now? DCL would at least have him on their books if things did look up. But it was just stupid this happening now.

Tear gas was what was needed. Drive the vermin out.

"Finished," Angie mimed at him. He lifted an earphone. "Look, I've finished."

"Good."

"Well look at it then - what do you think?"

"Very nice. Really good. No, I mean it, it's lovely. Great. C'mon, let's go to bed."

"In a minute. I want to see the end of this first."

"Why? You were doing your bloody pictures a minute ago. It's crap anyway, I've seen it before."

"Well I haven't."

"Watch it then, I'm going to bed."

He refilled his glass and went out

"There's no need to be like that..." But the door had closed.

He'd only just got into bed when she came in. She got undressed and into bed.

"Why are you in such a bad mood?" she asked, soothingly.

He was all hunched back and closed shoulders.

"I'm not. You go back and watch the film if you

want!"

"It's just nice to sit and watch a film together sometimes."

Together. That word again.

"Well I'm not stopping you..."

"That's not what I- meant..."

They never seemed to touch outside of bed. It irritated Tom when she wanted to cuddle or hold hands. He'd laugh or call her a 'nympho', but she didn't mean it that way - just touching, watching a stupid film with their arms round each other. Perhaps she was immature to like that, or the idea of that. Yes, Ralph had definitely been very immature.

She ventured a touch on the raised curve of his shoulders.

"Sorry," she said. She snuggled closer. He turned around and kissed her quickly on the mouth then pulled open her shirt, got most of one breast into his mouth and squeezed and massaged the other in his hand. It hurt more than anything, but she kept quiet and then he pushed her shirt out of the way and got inside her after a few attempts. She wasn't nearly ready but that was how he seemed to like it. She moaned and gasped - it hurt when it was like that - he kept his eyes shut and broke into a sweat when he'd come.

He lay with his head on her breast but she knew better than to stroke his hair or back so she rested her hands on his shoulders. His breathing returned to normal then he sighed and rolled away from her.

"I might not get that contract after all it looks

like," he said after a while.

"What's that?"

"That renovation job Pearce has put to me. Everything was going okay but then a whole pile of bloody squatters screw it up."

"What did they do?"

"They live there for Christ's sake!"

"Is that bad?"

"Well of course it is – we can't do the damn job if they're there, crawling about all over the place. We'd be had up for 'endangering life' - though I can't see why. We'd be doing everyone a big favour. Pass the ash-tray."

"Why don't they just move them out? Or go when they're not there."

Tom looked at her as if she had asked whether the earth was maybe flat after all which was how Arthur had looked at him earlier in the day when Tom had asked the exact same question.

"Because," he said, irritably patient, "they keep coming back before we can get it done. Things have to be booked with contractors in advance – we don't know when they're 'not there'. Or we throw one lot out and another lot swarm out of the sewers and put the kettle on. We'd have to get the law in, that can take weeks and you know what that means."

Angie didn't know - there was no way she could have known, but he got to roll his eyes in exasperation.

He also sighed impatiently; glad to have an outlet for his anger.

"Money. Contracts and everything. Time equals money on this one, the margins are tight as to whether they go for it or not and this could be the last straw. They shelve it - I'm out. Got it?"

"It'll be alright," she said. But that wasn't what he wanted. How could she possibly understand? Tom stubbed out his cigarette, removed the ashtray and rolled over onto his back. She felt cold where he'd been lying and turned to cuddle up to him.

"Where is this place anyway?"

"Other side of the river. Wild Rose Court. Two houses – one for nice luxury flats, one for demolition – mustn't have too many or the price'll go down."

He closed his eyes.

Angie said nothing.

*

Meanwhile, because of the sudden glut of available cash due to the interest rates dropping, a lot was happening around the country and the globe. There was, for example, suddenly a lot of building projects starting at the same time. They had been 'on hold' for years but the recent upturn had given many the go ahead. People had been employed, machinery bought and feverish activity begun.

Chapter 8

The news arrived just after Carol got back from London; Dorothy had opened the letter and headed for the nearest phone box with the big news.

She was offered the job!

She had applied for it and it was hers. Had she expected that? What had she expected? But she couldn't accept it. Not after all that. She couldn't handle it. Ken was right - The Big City. She couldn't cope with that. Stupid.

It wasn't as if she had expected to get it, was it?

But she had.

"I knew you'd crack it love," was her dad's reaction, giving her a hug, "and don't you worry," he enthused, "we'll fix you up. You'll be kitted out like any of them city types and we'll be down to see you and Dot before you know it." She noticed his eyes looked pink above the forced smile.

"You're going to take it then?" was her mum's. Her eyes looked wary.

"It is what I wanted. It'll be a start."

"There's nothing for them round here love. She'll be set up down there. She doesn't want to stay here for ever."

"I don't know what Ken'll say about it. A nice steady young lad like that and you flitting off to London. I don't know," her mum shook her head.

"Your decision love," said her dad.

"Thanks dad. I'm going to give Ken a ring and talk about."

"Right you are. Come on. We'll let them sort it out."

They went into the other room, Carol could hear their voices exchanging whispered fervent disagreement. She picked up the phone and dialled the well-known number.

Ken's mum answered. "Oh, hello dear. You've just missed him – he's down the Nag's. Haven't seen you since you got back. Are you coming over on Sunday?"

"Yes. I think so. I don't know yet," Carol stammered.

"Oh. Okay. I expect you'll let me know. See you then."

She said goodbye and put the phone down. That hadn't been very good. Carol always went over there on Sundays. Now his mum would know something was going on. She'd have had a fit if she'd thought her son was about to be finished with. Finished with?

Carol realised that was what she had in mind and was amazed. But only amazed - there was nothing else there. She had been anticipating all kinds of wrenching emotions to set upon her at the prospect of leaving 'her' Ken. The idea of leaving home was horrendous but she felt as if she could just quietly finish her relationship with him. As if it was something that was already finished. Or that had never really started. She had seen him when she had got back. She had realised she had not missed him much at all.

The barman at the pub answered and she heard him call out for "Ken' and tell him 'the missus' was on the phone. Carol could hear the familiar murmur and hum of darts night at the pub and thought she recognised a few voices. Then the phone was picked up.

"Carol? Where are you?"

"At home..."

"Are you coming down? There's a crowd down here. The girls are a bit outnumbered. Can you get here?"

"Well I was going to have an early night. Still feeling a bit tired."

"Don't be so boring girl! Come on..."

"I think London wore me out quite a bit. I'm not recovered yet." That was a lie, it had been days – she felt fine. Why was she lying and sidestepping into the subject?

"Oh aye. But you'll feel better after a few jars and some chat won't you. You can have a night in tomorrow - I'm going out with 'the lads'."

"I've just heard from London today actually. About that job."

"Oh yeah? You never told me how that interview went."

Because you never even asked, she wanted to say, *all you wanted to do was go and see that awful film.*

"I got it."

"What?"

"The job. I got it. And," she took a breath, "I want to accept it."

Her voice was flat and small.

"You kidding?"

"No."

Why did he think she was kidding? Was it so hard to believe she'd succeeded in something? She found it hard to believe. Why was that?

There was a silence at the other end of the line. She pictured him biting his upper lip, the way he did when something went wrong. Was he going to congratulate her?

"So what you going to do? Quieten down in here, I'm trying to talk!" he shouted to the pub.

"I'm not sure."

"What do you mean, 'not sure'?" His voice went quiet now. He wouldn't want the others to hear this, she thought. "You're not thinking of taking it? I mean alright, you've proved your point and we're all very impressed and all that, but you're not actually thinking of taking it? You'd have to move down there."

"I know."

There was another pause.

"I'm coming around there now and we're going to talk this one out properly."

"No Ken..." she wanted to celebrate with mum and dad first and have time to think things out a bit...

"Don't 'no Ken' me. I'll be round in ten minutes."

The phone clicked and burred at her. She went into the living room but she still felt cold. Her parents were waiting and had the sherry out in three glasses.

"We're right behind you, love. Here's to you." They all drank. It felt so awkward though. She'd not been away from home before for more than a couple of nights.

"Ken's coming around."

"Is he?" She saw them exchange glances.

"Well he can have a glass of sherry and a bit of cake. I'll fetch it out. Get another glass, Neil. I expect they'll want to talk."

She went out to fetch the irrelevant cake.

"Well you just remember," Neil lifted out another glass from the cupboard, "he's a nice enough lad, but it's your life, Carol. That's all I'll say. Don't let him or anyone bully you into anything. Yes?"

"Thanks dad." He didn't give advice very often but he obviously knew what was going on.

Her mum came back with the cake.

"That sounds like him now. Come on, Neil. Let them sort it out for themselves."

Before she closed the door behind them though, her mum held it open for a minute and said quietly to Carol, "Me and your dad are right behind you. Remember, you're only young once. No good getting carried away with all this career nonsense if you don't get settled first. Then you can look around... That's all I'm saying..."

There were voices in the kitchen and she went out and Ken came in.

He wasn't either smiling or frowning. He looked wary. He sat down, not next to her as he usually did, but across the room.

They exchanged 'hello's'.

"Like some cake?"

"Thanks, no," and he waved away the glass of sherry.

"Carol," he said, she looked at him, "you know what's going to happen if you go down there, don't you?"

No, it occurred to her, *and that's exactly why I want to go.* But she didn't say it.

"There's weekends," she said.

"Oh yeah, there's weekends alright, but I live here Carol and I'm not the sort to stop in every night 'til the weekend comes round am I?"

She looked at her glass. It was empty but she kept hold of it. He always looked too big in their lounge.

"You could come down."

"Yes, I could, and how much would that cost us? You know what I'm talking about, it happens all the time when people start messing about and moving around. And how would I know what you were doing down there eh? You might meet someone else as well. And then what? I'm not going to be kept waiting here while you're jetting off round the bright lights with

71

everyone you meet. That's not the sort of girl I want is it?"

"I'm not going to..."

"I don't know that, do I?"

Carol realised that neither did she and found the idea rather fascinating. She hadn't thought about this before.

"I don't know why you got all this into your head in the first place. I'll be earning enough for both of us by the time we clinch it, but then you have to bug... go off to London after some stupid job. It's that stupid Edwards woman, isn't it? With her bloody ideas? I'm sorry I let you go to that place now, I should have known better..."

He was standing now. His voice was raised slightly. He hated not getting his own way.

But then, so did she.

"It's got nothing to do with her, or anyone, it's me who wants to do it. And you've known that for ages. Before we got engaged."

"Well? And doesn't that mean anything to you? How long have we been going out? A year? How can we be engaged with me here and you there? You're not the only girl round here you know. And you're not getting any younger."

"Nor you..." She didn't say anything about what she suspected of what happened on his 'nights out with the lads'. The clues she'd found in the car.

"Yeah well, don't you worry about me; you know what happens to career girls, don't you? They're too busy to meet anybody, that's what and they end up on the shelf and who'll want you then, eh?"

He was right, every word. She'd known it, somehow, all her life. She couldn't deny it.

But then she remembered someone. Carol stood up and walked calmly over to the door.

"Well, I'm going to bed now. So you'll have to excuse me."

"Hang on, you can't go now. Have you changed your mind on London or not? I'll go when we've sorted this one out."

"There's nothing to sort out. I might never have this chance again and all I'll do is stay here and get older. You don't want me to go - but it isn't me you want, is it? You just want someone. Someone there. In your life. Well, it's my life and I'm going. There's nothing to sort!"

Courage seemed to fail her and she opened the door. Her parents' voices from the kitchen stopped as they heard the lounge door open.

She fetched Ken's jacket. He stared at her as he put it on. She looked past him.

"I'll call again when you've calmed down a bit," he said. He turned to go, "But you think on what I've said. G'night Mrs Prempton, Mr Prempton," he nodded. "I'll see you again. That's for sure!"

He looked hard at Carol as he said this, then he was gone. They heard the car pull out and drive off.

Carol was on the point of running out after him and saying sorry, sorry, sorry, I didn't mean it – and getting it all back to normal again and never mind about the stupid job.

But the urge to do so just wasn't quite strong enough.

Her mum opened her mouth to speak but Carol walked past her and up the stairs. Her dad went back to the telly and the cake and poured his wife another sherry. "It's her life, love," he murmured. Her mum nodded.

Later though, when they were all watching television, a few gremlins came and sat on Carol's shoulder, looking for weak points in her armour. She was on her own now, despite her parents sitting just across the room.

But again, as before, she only had to remember someone who'd done more than anyone, more than Carol herself and all the Mrs Edwards's in the world, to get Carol the chance she needed: Dorothy, her sister. Dorothy was living in London now where her husband's job had taken her, in the elusive Cambridge Walk, but while she was here she had helped Carol with her studies and encouraged her to keep going.

She'd been married nearly two years now.

Was it really two years ago already?

Dorothy had been twenty then. It had been all forget-me-not sky, smiles, pastels and greys with an up-dated ceremony and an exchange of rings but still the mothers wept, and Carol too at the loss of a sister.

Dot had looked marvellous of course and 'such a nice young man' as everyone kept saying and, "Your turn next," they all gloated until Carol smiled, blushed and wanted to either sink through the floor or kill somebody.

She wondered though. Dorothy had known Roy since youth-club. Carol was already 17 and there was no-one in sight. Most of her ex-schoolmates were 'going steady'. She'd expected, or had been expected, to meet someone at the evening classes but they were mostly girls and swotting for her exams had taken up so many other evenings.

At the wedding, looked forward to over the months of preparation, she just felt out of place. The only single girl there, or so it seemed, and everyone in couples or groups of friends she didn't know. She sat with her parents and some aunties and danced with some uncles and junior cousins and envied Dorothy: a laughing cascade of white amongst the throng of old friends and loved ones; her brand-new, ready-made family and her joking, slightly drunk husband who had asked Carol for a dance and teased her about her boyfriend-less state.

The friend who Carol had brought with her had brought along her boyfriend and spent the entire disco-reception apparently swapping secrets with him. The groom's friends had seemed like creatures from another world and all seemed just that bit too old or a bit too young to be seen dancing with a 'kid sister'. But it was Dorothy's day and Carol had kept smiling for her, to hide how out of it she felt.

Dorothy had kissed her goodbye and driven off to her new life – in a cloud of confetti and carbon-monoxide. She had thrown her bouquet to Carol to the approval and amusement of many. Some 'jocular' comments were made and she'd winced behind her smile which was beginning to hurt.

After they'd gone, some had taken to serious

drinking and some went home, others danced. The 'parents of the bride' had to stay until the end so she spent a lot of time dancing with more uncles and meeting people who said, "So you're the little sister," and, "When is it your turn?" and very little else. She'd sought refuge outside on one occasion only to find a neighbour entwined with someone not his wife in the shrubbery so she'd pretended not to see and ducked back into the club past Mr and Mrs Wright who were having another row in the hallway and into the Ladies – which seemed to be the only place to which to escape.

She spent quite some time in there pretending to fix her almost non-existent make-up. She kept going back for another check-up when she felt she had blushed and stammered enough.

Unfortunately, after one nerve-racking foray into the wall of strangers and tipsy uncles she was just a bit too quick on the retreat and a woman who'd just gone in when Carol was leaving was still there when she returned.

"Hello," she said. "It's Carol isn't it? That was a bit quick - is the Press gang getting to you or have you got the trots?"

"What?"

"The Press Gang? You know," she was fixing her fabulous looking hair into order, "the Born-again Couple-Cult out looking for converts? They're always at their worst at weddings. It's their Big Thing. Poor sods. It isn't mine, thank God! Don't let them corner you, that's all."

"It is a bit like that."

"A bit? They'd marry you to the vicar to make the numbers tidy. Or shoot you."

"It makes me feel weird."

The woman laughed. "So? *Be* weird! Never did me any harm."

She didn't look as if anything could. Carol tried to guess how old she was.

"Are you married?"

"Oh god, don't you start. No, I bloody well ain't! Been there, done that and no thanks! But if they make you feel weird, get your own back... when they ask you when you're getting married, ask them when they're getting divorced. Or try and get them to talk about something else. They can't handle that. Most of them, it's all they think about. Perverts! At least if you stay single you give them all an alternative topic of conversation - much needed too. Drat, now I've smudged!"

She had finished brushing her hair and was smoothing colour on her eyelids. She stopped to get out a tissue and caught sight of Carol's face in the mirror. She laughed again.

"What a face! This is a wedding not a wake. You're meant to enjoy it!"

She finished her makeup, took Carol by the arm and steered her out of the refuge.

"Don't let them get you down. You're entitled to enjoy yourself without being given a contract. Don't give in to them. 'Oh look,' they'll say, 'Carol's so unhappy 'cos she hasn't got a fellah,' and they'll make sure of that. Nuts to 'em! C'mon, let's confuse them.

There's a group of lads about your age, bored out of their minds. Go and have a dance and enjoy yourself. They're too shy and hopeless to ask you so you'll have to do it. Go on, I'm watching you - can't spend your life in a toilet! Go on; show them you're not a kid!"

She gave Carol a gentle push towards the table.

The word 'kid' sang in Carol's ears and kept her going, though her face was burning. She advanced into the enemy territory where she stood, dumbstruck among the blue and grey uniforms. What could she say?

One of the enemy looked up from their conference around the table.

She hadn't been able to see the juvenile acne from a distance. Then she saw that they were playing a surreptitious game of cards under the table out of sight. They looked up, startled at being discovered. As out of place as she was.

Carol dug her voice up from where it had scuttled to hide.

"Would you like to dance-?"

It wasn't clear whether she was asking all of them or the table itself but she couldn't look any of them in the eye. Oh God what had she done? Were her parents watching? They'd be shocked.

"Yeah sure, thanks," one said. Two had half-risen, one had blushed and the others just stared, nonplussed - all uncomfortable in their finery and wary of her in hers, but one was quicker and they went onto the dance floor. The music was loud enough for them not to have to bother with small talk. They just danced, avoiding each other's eyes. She saw her new friend who smiled and winked at her over someone's shoulder.

She winked back feeling very worldly. And it was a good record so she relaxed and started to enjoy herself...

A month later, Dorothy had had to go into hospital. 'Women's Troubles' her mother had called it but she'd looked more unhappy than Carol had ever seen her. A while later, Carol had gone to stay with them in their new house on the other side of town - Dorothy was up and about but there was something else wrong that had nothing to do with hospitals.

Roy was out nearly every night she was there, or so it seemed. Dorothy was tired all the time and the friendly chit-chat she was used to at home was completely missing. Roy was more or less polite but obviously didn't like her being there. Was she the problem? She'd suggested an early return home but Dorothy had looked so upset and had asked her to stay so insistently that she'd felt ashamed of thinking herself unwelcome in her sister's house.

She didn't tell Dot that Roy made her feel unwelcome, or that she didn't like the way he leered at her or made snide comments about, 'sweet seventeen and never been'.

"He likes his beer and his mates and his nights out," was all Dorothy had said once, after the door had closed. "He always did. No reason for him to change."

Except that she had changed status from 'the missus' to 'the wife' nothing much had changed.

Except that 'girls' had often been included in night's out and wives were not, nothing much had changed. Dorothy still went along once a week and got together with others for 'girls' nights out, but those other nights; when she and Roy had gone out together alone, just the two of them, had more or less stopped.

"What's the point? I can cook a meal just as well here. The TV's in there. We can sleep together whenever we want and no one bats an eyelid (Carol had blushed at her mentioning such a thing), so why go out? And this house takes paying for, you know."

A few months, was that all? From seeing each other two or three times a week, occasional weekend trips and special occasions, they were now together every supper and breakfast, all the hours between and every weekend when, instead of the countryside, they went to the superstore and instead of the cinema, they watched television. For hours. Instead of mates ringing up, people left them to entertain each other, not wanting to 'intrude'.

Only a few months after all the romance and excitement of the wedding? 'See you then' and a quick peck over the breakfast dishes, if that? Dorothy had caught her sister's expression one morning.

"Aye well, that's how it goes. It's not all passion and lace you know."

Another time, Carol had come in from town and Roy had walked past her and upstairs without a look or a word and she'd found Dorothy on the verge of tears in the living room.

She'd said, "It's alright Carol, just a little tiff that's all. All part of married life..." Then, a little later, when

Carol had fetched some tea, "I wish, I wish..."

"Go on, Dorothy, anything at all..." Carol had promised.

Dorothy had almost laughed at that, but then it had caught in her throat and choked into a sob. And then, in a rush, "I just wish there was something to look forward to, that's all. This was it, wasn't it? For years. Not much after all, was it? Not much. Big joke." Her voice got high pitched and trapped sounding.

Roy came down, called, "I'm off out," from the hallway and left.

Carol didn't have the know-how or the words to cope. Her mother would have told *Dot not to be so silly* and would have had her drying her eyes in no time but that didn't seem appropriate somehow.

Dot sniffed and dried her eyes. She didn't cry easily. They weren't a demonstrative family. Her face was all blotchy.

"How's it all going with these courses of yours then?" she had brought her cracked, choky voice under control.

"Fine. It's going fine. It's great." Dorothy had helped Carol with the assignments and had spent time going over things with her to help her get on the course.

"Well, you keep up with them, you hear me?"

"I hear you. Of course I'll keep up with them."

"Don't you go dropping out - you got that?"

Carol nodded.

"That's all I'll say - I'm not saying it's bad, it isn't but…"

She took a deep breath and the sigh seemed to take up her whole being and there was nothing to be said.

"You keep up with those courses, that's all. And are you on the pill?"

Horribly embarrassed, Carol burned red and shook her head. Surely Dot wasn't suggesting that she would…?

"Well get on it! Use other things as well of course, the pill only stops babies - and not even that 100% - and I should know. So just you make sure. And they won't get rid of it unless you can prove you're round the twist or something or can fork out enough dosh. Some hope of that!"

She was talking to herself more than to Carol who couldn't really follow.

Carol had never felt she wanted to do… that with anyone anyway. Not with anyone she'd had a date with at any rate. Not with this Ken she had just met either. She had never wondered why this was and just assumed it would work out.

It did for everyone else, didn't it?

Dorothy looked at her. "I can't have any more children now."

Carol looked away. The word 'more' made things clear and understanding suddenly hit her.

"Rum'un that isn't it, considering? C'mon, let's have some of those biscuits while old misery guts is out."

Then she'd ruffled Carol's hair - which she hadn't done for years. "You keep your options open, don't worry about me. I'll sort this somehow. C'mon, another cuppa would be nice…"

The film had ended. Carol came back into the present. "Well I didn't think much of that," her dad said. "Do you want this left on? I'm off to bed." Her mum and dad tidied away the remains of supper.

"G'night - don't be too late — these businesswomen need their shut-eye!"

"Go on with you. See you tomorrow."

She'd write back to Mr Pearce in the morning telling him she accepted his offer of employment and write to Dorothy as well, telling her about it. Dorothy would invite her to stay at her house — she'd memorized the address this time - and that would be great.

*

Meanwhile, as a lot of building projects were reaching completion at the same time in some places, there seemed to be a bit of a warning dip in the prices for which these buildings could be sold. There was suddenly a threat there may eventually be too many coming on the market. Interest rates seemed to be rising again as there was going to be a shortage of the money that was once saved so carefully so there was a bit of pressure to get a quick return on the investments. More meetings were held. Some of them at Carmichael's (DCL) Ltd.

Chapter 9

"You like things being closed down then, do you?" he said conversationally. "Don't like hospitals much?" but the man had gone, his back disappearing into the crowd and his snide, unoriginal comment lost on the chill air.

Ralph hunched his shoulders against the cold and the indifferent world and switched the collecting tin from hand to hand. He hadn't got many stickers left so it was going quite well. He liked helping out when there was a campaign. It made a change from busking, pulling pints or cleaning. It was good to keep company with others sometimes who saw the world from a similar angle.

"I'd love to get back to work - along with three million others like me!"

He couldn't see who Anna was shouting at but he could guess the stupid comment she must have just received. He grinned at her until she saw him and grimaced back. It was no good glowering at people – that wouldn't help fill the collecting tins. It was no good not shouting back either - the abuse got you down until you felt like giving up and didn't have the confidence to shout into the void. A lot of people gave though and that made it worthwhile. People were glad to see someone was at least 'having a go' against the prevailing gloom. Even if it was only the workers at the local bread factory in this little corner of the city. People stopped at the little trestle tables to sign the petition.

Ralph noticed that he and Anna and the others in the Support Our Breadmakers were moving in a kind of dance from one foot to the other - in order to keep warm, avoid passers-by who refused to see you and to sort of wind up the energy for another assault on the world. If they broke into a song and dance routine would they do better, he wondered?

Anna was in full flood with someone who'd just asked her why she wasn't collecting for something 'worthwhile', when she noticed Ralph had come over and was hovering for attention. The 'worthwhile' moved away - still not having given.

"I think we should move," said Ralph, suddenly.

"Police again?"

"No, but it's not very good here is it?"

"We're doing alright here aren't we?"

Anna glanced at the others to see if they were lifting the table to move too.

"I just want to move," he said, creativity failing him.

"Fair enough. Lead on."

Ralph quickly turned to go but it was too late.

"Ralph! Ralph!" It sounded like a dog.

It was a dog.

"Oh, hello Allan!" Ralph feigned both surprise and pleasure.

"How's things?"

It was Allan and Caroline, arm in arm.

"Couldn't be better. Still pushing dissent, I see? Enjoyed our drink the other night, must do it again some time... Oh, hello Anna."

Anna's face lit into a warm day of a smile.

"Hello! You're just in time – we were just leaving - like to make a contribution?"

She held out the tin with a happy expectant smile to Caroline - who looked confused. Allan looked downright scared but soon recovered.

"What's it for? Oh, I see. They'll have to close though won't they? They don't make a profit," he said, knowledgeably.

"That's right, Allan," Anna smiled sweetly, "they make bread, hence: bakery. As in 'Save Our'. See?" She pointed brightly to the sticker. "Like to make a contribution?"

She turned to Caroline, "Some of them have got children – the bakers that is and they are awfully cute. Just a bit poor. Be a bit poorer if they lose. So...?" She proffered the tin again.

Caroline glared at her. "Of course, love to!" she said. Allan reached for his wallet and Caroline rummaged in the designer shoulder-bag, her designer hair falling forward over her designer face.

She dug out an unusual looking purse and counted

the edges of a roll of notes of an unfamiliar shade. She carefully eased out one of these and folded it tight to push through the slot in the top of the tin. That'd show her. But Anna was staring at the rest of the roll in Caroline's other, mittened hand.

"What? Only one? What about that lot?"

The ingratitude hit Caroline's smile like a slap. She looked at Anna and her nostrils seemed to flare - a very interesting effect which Anna hadn't seen before on a human.

Caroline's composure returned and she looked away, slipping her arm through Allan's. Ralph seemed to be counting the two coins he had in his hand rather carefully.

"Thank you ever so," said Anna, brightly, and moved away.

"Well, Ralph, how's the house working out? I thought she'd gone?"

"She's back. It's fine. You been on holiday?"

"Oh, it was simply super," Caroline wanted to answer this.

"It was amazing!" she enthused at Ralph. "A totally enriching experience. Just a quick break but we got right away. We avoided all the usual routes and the tourist areas, you know..." Ralph didn't know but he nodded anyway. "It can be all *so* predictable, don't you think? We found these villages, so unspoilt, *so* interesting, *ama*-zing people, so welcoming - terribly poor, but *very* rich in other ways - you know?"

Ralph didn't have a clue but he was always willing to learn so he nodded again.

"I think it's important to remember that," she said, looking at the collecting tin for the strike fund, "hardship can produce a different kind of wealth, you know, the spirit can rise above it. I thought it was wonderful. I really learned a lot."

"You did?" Ralph said, hopefully.

"Oh yes, I'm sure if you went there you would realise about poverty."

"I expect if I could afford to, I'd need to," Ralph agreed. Caroline beamed at him benignly, the irony lost on the autumn air.

"Poverty is so picturesque isn't it – from a distance?" offered Anna, helpfully.

Caroline glared at her. "Well no one I met there had a chip on their shoulder!" Anna hadn't heard that one for a while.

"Er, chip on my shoulder?" Anna slapped her own forehead with the palm of her hand, her face a picture of sudden enlightenment, "Of course! That's it! You keep giving us crap and we just keep on not liking it! What's wrong with us?!" She held out her arms in exasperation with the world and shook her head in wonderment. Caroline looked like she'd swallowed a wasp; Allan pretended to be adjusting his watch; Ralph grinned – noting how good at drams Anna really was.

"It's not like that anymore," Caroline intoned. "My father is rich – as you know - and one of his wealthiest shareholders is coloured: Adam Singleton, and he's darker than you - so you've no excuse now! He's reached the top!"

"Black!" said Anna. "We've not been coloured in. You're right, of course; you're dad's a rich guy, so's this Adam What-his-name – so, I see, all everyone just needs to do is to get rich too! Sorted! Everyone at the bottom of the pyramid just needs to climb up to the top!" Anna demonstrated this rising up with her collecting tin. "Then we'd all be at the top! Easy!" Anna frowned at the space beneath the raised tin as if she'd spotted a problem. "You don't know much about pyramids, do you – there'd be nobody holding the top bit up - if we were all in the top bit?"

Caroline looked blank. Anna gave it up as a lost cause and went back to asking passers by for support for the bakers.

"Did you go on holiday Ralph?" Allan changed the subject, tactfully - and pointedly.

"Yeah, Britain. Nice. Well, some of it, y'know. Mostly London actually. Round here mainly as it happens. Enriching experience mind you. I'm at the Cornfield now and again, and some others… You'll have to stop by."

They thanked him graciously then moved off arm in arm.

"You be careful mixing with that type," said Anna, watching, "you never know what you might pick up. You should talk to him. You can't stand aside and watch your mate being turned into an idiot."

"Back into an idiot, you mean. Remember, I've known him for years. He was alright for a while at college but that was a blip. Normal service has now been resumed."

"So, how come you're still mates with him?" said

Anna suspiciously.

"Habit. I have got worse ones. I'll tell you about them when you're old enough. And the free drinks. And the odd meal. Not that I believe in using people. But if they force it on me... Anyway, he's doing alright for himself."

"He's sold out!"

"He was never in. Believe me. He had a brief flirtation with being a human being - slumming it at college when he had to share with me. I think he was humouring me – us - old school mates and all that, but he never took to it. Honestly. It wasn't natural for him. It was making him ill."

"Well it's sad. He'll be scratching his armpits and swinging about in trees next."

"So long as he keeps chucking me down the odd bunch of bananas I won't mind. He'll never change unless it suits him for the moment. I've seen him in a range of guises - this one's relatively okay. Caroline's off her head - but she does want to change the world, but only into a fwuffy-ickle toy shop. She wants to make it a better place – but without changing anything – a tricky kind of maths. I'm dying to see how far she gets with it."

"She's got the clothes for it. You can't look that 'alternative' without owning a mint. Does look good," Anna begrudged.

Anna was determined not to be 'the hurt and jilted' woman.

"Alternative my arse!" Ralph put in. "Chip on your shoulder? Blimey! That's going back a bit, isn't it?

You black people," Ralph parodied, "No sense of humour – you should smile and be happy and enjoy abuse!"

Anna smiled, ruefully. "And be like Adam Singleton – whoever he is! At least she says it out loud! Let's go and hand these in and go home for a cup of tea. We could do the fly-posting tonight. What does she see in him, I wonder?"

"A bit of rough? Who knows? Hidden depths?" suggested Ralph.

"Oh, he's got hidden depths alright," agreed Anna. "So's a cesspit."

"Well there you are. What did you see in him?"

"Nothing. But I thought there'd be no harm in looking."

They walked on in silence for a while.

"I thought he was a teacher when I met him," she remembered, "so I guessed he was all kind and creative and all that rot. We all make mistakes."

"He's landed on his feet, mind," said Ralph, wistfully.

"Never mind. Ralph, it'll be open-season on buskers and barmen next and all the jet-set will be after you. Smothering you in lust and champagne."

"I'd just have to put on a brave face and try and cope. I'd hate to disappoint them," said Ralph, heroically.

"You wouldn't sell out though, would you Ralph? You wouldn't turn ape for the price of a penthouse and a Porsche would you?"

For an answer, Ralph hunched over, scuttled sideways to a doorway, gibbering and grinning at frightened passers-by and scratching fervently under his arms.

He was alright really, despite some of the company he kept. She'd asked him to come along to the collection that morning for the baker shop and been surprised when he'd said yes. He'd been in other campaigns before, she was surprised to find. She had always thought he was a bit of a prat with his obsession with music and so on but he was okay really.

They dropped off the tins, collected some posters for the rally and headed home. They went halves for the glue at a shop on the way.

There was a brown envelope on the doorstep of the squat when they returned.

"More fan-mail? How do your adoring hordes always track you down?"

"Well this one's threatening to take us to court if we don't vacate premises."

"That's code for 'Be Mine or I'll kill myself'. One day I'll be coming home to begging letters, hysterical fan-mail and death-threats all over the doormat. Then I'll know I've made it."

"Meanwhile, you'll have to start saving for a doormat. Not to mention a door. Who's that?"

Anna was frowning across the road to the other house. "I haven't seen him before. The surveying lot don't usually dress like that."

"He doesn't look much like a squatter either."

"Ee, not like us, not from round here. We'll have

to get a set of net curtains to peer round at him."

"Could be the owner?"

"Don't stereotype him. He could be an ex-hippie on a nostalgia trip... He could be searching for a runaway daughter...or wife..."

"...or running away... from his daughter... and his wife."

"Well he seems harmless enough."

"Said the villagers, as the leper appeared in the distance."

"Don't be sick. Better get to work."

"See you about 12 then?"

They went their separate ways.

Chapter 10

Across the road, Arthur Pearce, a minor manager of a minor department from Carmichael and Sons (DCL) Ltd was enjoying himself. These were the shells - the shells of a past age of elegance, long hatched and flown. He'd crossed over to the second, less dilapidated one in search of further delights from the past.

The first house, where Anna and Ralph had just arrived, had revealed some beautiful plasterwork and two fireplaces that looked original and, most important, because the least expected, in the broken-down one-time summerhouse in the back garden which he had had to get to by clambering through the damp, cobwebbed horror of the ground-floor - was an intact, original stained-glass roof. It seemed to glow in the early evening autumn sun. All but a few panes were intact, protected by a mulch of dirt and leaves built up-over the years - so many years - yet it was still there. Put there by skilled hands you just couldn't get any more for some reason. Arthur had stood engrossed for several minutes in the overgrown walled garden, thinking of past times.

Remnants of exotic plants were still discernible amongst the ragged, weed-ridden undergrowth.

Now he had crossed over the street to the second remnant.

Arthur looked at this second house from the gate. The late afternoon sun blazed the ancient bricks to brightness where they showed their haggard worthy faces peering through the plaster's ragged edges. The tunnel of the hall, beyond the heavy doorstep, that had withstood centuries of welcomes, was a deep grey of shadow with zebras of light striped across it from the doors and windows on either side.

In the pale stripes of light, lay neglect in ugly shapes and shadows fallen plaster and chunks of wood and dust and dust and dust.

The door was open.

Arthur walked through the tiny chaos of the front garden and went in.

Silence hung and a soft warm smell and shadows cluttered the dark. Here the soft-footed servant came, across the polished hall to answer the early morning callers' tasteful chime, to take their hats or calling cards, bow slightly at the waist, show them to the drawing-room perhaps. She'd glide away, happy at a job well done, to bustle happy, fresh-faced maids in crimped black and white and dimples to bring in the refreshments and the wine to serve the little cakes, fresh baked that day by a vast and red-faced cook. Ah then!

And the Master of the house - kindly but standing no nonsense from anyone - would come down, wearing a dark, well-pressed suit - rather like Arthur's -

with a watch on a chain perhaps, with a long moustache and a top-hat, and his wife quiet and pretty and content doing embroidery and things. The children with their nanny, and the cook downstairs with the grouse and the quail and the pigs' heads and big fruit puddings - fruit of course from the garden - well-tended by a team of honest, hardworking gardeners with moustaches and nicotine-stained fingers which touched their caps when the Master was seen and no mistake... Ah then - before everyone had started getting out of their place and being unsatisfied...

And here - the first room on the left, with its carved fireplace – probably now in need of a good sweep, was obviously the music-room where the family would have sat for hours, listening happily to the spinet or harp or to the master reading from the Bible on Sundays or passages from... Chaucer or somebody. Arthur drew himself up to his full height like an orator - then he would summon the butler to bring in the tea, Arthur raised his arm to beckon.

"Who the fuck are you?" Arthur's heart stopped.

A black and white and dimpled maid? Hardly. The light fell behind the figure which was in dreadful silhouette at the bottom of the stairs. It had a knife in its hand.

"What do you think you're doing?" it said.

"Oh my gosh." Arthur's heart raced.

"You looking for someone or what?"

"No, no, it's quite alright... I thought for a moment..."

"Well, what do you want?"

This certainly wasn't the butler.

"There's nothing to steal if that's what you've come for..."

He, a thief! The very idea!

"My dear young lady, I do assure you..."

"And this is a good knife if you've other ideas."

Arthur stepped back a little.

"I'm not a thief and I am not a... a... you misunderstand me. I am merely interested in old buildings, stranded by the tides of history as these are. I was merely looking around this quiet backwater of our heritage."

"You some kinda nut?"

"Actually, you're trespassing," Arthur said, asserting himself.

He would have said more, perhaps, and debated the ins and outs of housing law with her but then he saw the knife move. He changed his mind and started backing towards the door. You couldn't be too careful with these crouchers - desperate lot, communists, some of them - moving in, taking over, wrecking homes and living in filth, all sleeping together and swallowing drugs all day long. My God, he was probably standing in a dark hallway with a mentally deranged person with a knife! He raised a hand to emphasise his next words.

"Don't you come any closer!" Liz snapped, misinterpreting the gesture. "There are six more people upstairs and they've got guns, you stay right there!"

"I'm going, alright? I'm going," Arthur spoke clearly and slowly. "I- don't- want- any- trouble. I- am- not- repeat- *not* an hallucination- understand? I- am- a- real- person. Do- you- read- me? No need to wave that knife about!"

He sounded rather like a Dalek. Liz was rather confounded, not having had to deal with a Dalek before.

He didn't seem to be getting through. The strange woman stared at him. She was probably incapable of rational thought. He had to keep calm at all costs. Back slowly...

He reached the door... footsteps were behind him. He whirled round to fend off this new attack, his arms raised instinctively...

It was a monster.

"Everything alright, Liz? What's this? Trouble?" the monster asked, walking up to the door.

"God knows, he just barged in here. Scared me to death. I think he's on something."

Arthur got past the apparition with the half-scalped, bloody-looking head - he had had no idea that hallucinations were so quickly contagious - and hurried back to his car, with a hideous, cold, pursued feeling scurrying up and down his spine.

A narrow escape!

He got the right key in the lock at last and slammed the door behind him and heaved a sigh of relief.

He hadn't been pursued by the two maniacs.

He wouldn't be doing that again in a hurry. He had no idea it could be so dangerous. It wasn't his job to evict them, thank goodness! It was such a lovely old house as well. They both were. Pity they weren't safe to explore properly.

He needed a good dinner and a pick-me-up after that. Clara wouldn't be back until tomorrow so the big house would be empty. There must be somewhere round here with a good menu and decent claret.

Liz and Reny watched the car roar away.

"Glad you got back just then, Reny," said Liz, "it's not safe around here these days."

Chapter 11

Anna got to 'The Bell' and walked round to the back entrance where great iron bins held the day's throw-outs from the restaurant side: shards, lumps, heaps and stains of leftovers leaked out from under the battered lids. Ice-cream, boxes of burgers, cod-fillets with parsley sauce, chocolate gateaux and peas seemed to have been the dish of the day. Something of less discriminating taste had fetched a dead something else out and dragged it with a garnish of potato and carrot peelings across to the bushes around the car park. It didn't take an Indian-tracker's skills to detect urban wildlife.

Anna stepped over the trail and went up the steps to the kitchen. It was already hot with steam.

"Hi, Mo. Hello, Agatha."

"Hello, luv."

"Oh look out, Mo, the reds are back. Stand by to defend yourself!" Aggie was holding a whisk and brandished it 'on guard' to Anna.

"What you gonna do?" asked Mo. "Make her into an omelette?"

The washing-up liquid bottle was empty and the 'sword-fight' Aggy's whisk vs. Anna's squeezy bottle - was just in its first skirmishes when the second-in-command came in. Aggy put down the whisk, picked up her notepad and dodged out to the restaurant.

Anna continued the sweep of her arm with the squeeze bottle and squirted some into the washing up sink and turned on the hot taps.

Jones, the second in command, looked puzzled.

"Enough of that," he said, deciding on vagueness. "I've told you. You watch your step, messing about. There's plenty more where... where... where's...?"

Exactly on cue, Reny arrived, carrying an empty crate. Both Anna and Mo knew that he had picked up that crate in the yard on his way in, but it was a good prop for a late entrance.

"And where've you been?" Jones looked at his watch.

"Down the cellar!" said Reny. Things like, 'where else would I have been?' and 'you couldn't possibly have thought I was late!' were written all over his face.

It was very convincing. He'd had plenty of practice.

"Well some more wine needs fetching up - the House Red..." Reny was gone, back through the door like the wind - to avoid having to hear again the inevitable, "and make it snappy!" which Jones called out after him.

Jones looked around the kitchen. No dishes yet. The bin had been emptied... but there must be something... of course, yes... "You get this floor swept ready instead of mucking about wasting time!" Anna left the wiping surfaces charade she had adopted to do something with the hot water in the absence of dishes and grabbed the broom.

Jones nodded over at Mo.

"Good evening Mr Erin."

"Good evening, Mr Jones."

Mo was leaning on the fridge eating a large cheese bap slowly.

This was his empire. He was chef. He didn't need to jump when middle-managers came in for a bit of square-bashing.

"Leave that," Mo said, when Jones had left and Anna was pretending to sweep the perfectly clean floor. "Aggies's just mopped it. He was just belly-aching."

"He's got the capacity for it," noted Anna, "he's got the most badly managed middle of any middle-manager I know."

"S'alright, Aggie, he's gone. Shall we have a cuppa? How's Joe? Any better?"

"Not so bad today. Doctor said the plaster can come off in a while but he won't be able to work for a while. He ate a good meal today anyway. That was something."

"Spoil him, you do," Mo finished his sandwich, uncovered a hat-like wonder of sugar and cream, seized a huge bag of cement-like substance in his raw-steak hands and started putting delicate finishing touches to a lacework of finest pink icing around the white daisies and blue roses he had created. "It's all this silver-service in bed what's done it, eh, Aggie?"

"Don't you be so cheeky."

"Are you wearing that to a wedding or is it for our tea-break?"

"Ho-bloody-ho and what tea-break? This magnificent - turn those steaks over Reno would you - this miraculous creation is for tonight's sweet trolley. There. Have a good look. You'll be hoovering it off the carpet tomorrow so see it in its glory while you can. Instead of the factory stuff. Cheaper, the Boss reckons. Gateaux de la Maison – or Our Cake if you prefer. The cheeky sod asked if I knew how to do it! There, finished. Come here, Reny, let's ice your spikes... No... hands on deck, we're in business!"

Anna worked here some evening and lunchtimes since finishing her course. It was well below the going rate for the job but it was all she could get. Reny was earning even less on his facade of a training 'Youth Employment Scheme'. He was learning to be a general dogsbody and was learning fast; his catering skills - now stretched as far as bin-emptying, crate-shifting and, on a good day, carrot-scraping.

He had an outlandish haircut – reminiscent of Punk's early years; one side thick, longish straightish - and completely haywire - this was the side he'd dyed red. Previously his hair had been peroxide blonde all over and the Boss had had a 'quiet word' with him about that, and his earrings. He had used the old 'the customers don't like it'/gives the place a bad name/doesn't do us any good, you know' routine.

Reny had figured out how much he liked the customers/who 'us' was/and how much good the place was doing him - then shaved off half the offending ruff and dyed the other half blood-red as a compromise. The Boss had said nothing more. It would affect Reny's references but he reckoned his 'catering' career wasn't going very far anyway, with or without references.

A light blue stack of dishes arrived for Anna: yellow rubber gloves, green liquid, white suds - hers was a colourful job.

Hot steam, cool bubbles, sensual too. The standing was the only problem: she usually did a few knee-bends during her shift and walked around the kitchen, getting in Mo's way, to ease her back a little. Agatha, nearly three times her age and on her feet all day, back and forth, had given her advice about discreetly flexing and stretching her leg muscles ("You on about it again, Aggie, you kinky bugger you? Leave the poor girl alone, you're corrupting her!") to keep the circulation going and to keep 'the varicose' away.

The kitchen was too busy now with orders coming through and Mo singing, fans whirring and the extractor humming and Mo swearing to have anything like a heart to heart with anybody. The excitement of moving plates from one pile, through hot water onto another pile soon lost its novelty appeal and the autumn dusk, beautiful on hillsides or in ancient woodlands of beech or oak, where it could be called 'the gloaming', became cramped and hideous in the yard outside where all times of year and day were distorted.

It was better to switch to 'ChAnnal' Five as Anna called it, and see what came up.

There'd been nothing in the theatre magazine she rifled through every week at the library again. Sod all in the columns either. There'd be Club parts now coming up with the season starting - all good experience but it was getting on for six months since the Centre had closed. That had been a good place, a high time - while it had lasted – only volunteer work but great experience in amongst the bar work... Six months ago already...

Saturday mornings had been the best, she remembered: thirty or so 'Under Fifteens' - very broadly translated - some determined to get to Broadway, others 'come to watch', some to try a new variety of trouble but most to get in out of the rain and boredom: Drama.

Drama it was: with no set syllabus, no exams and no-one to please but themselves. They had had mornings of, perhaps, Storytelling, Bodygames - 'Aye aye miss, what's that then?' – 'make-up' – the drawers at home robbed of their ten-year old deposits of fuschia and green, orange and pink and they found that felt-tip pens didn't wash off so well; 'Emotions' - 'When are we going to do some proper acting?' and, at last – 'Sketches' - what would happen if... and the whole world was theirs.

Then the decision was made somewhere to close the Centre down.

There had been some protests and sit-ins, brief ones, but although a lot of parents were also attending courses or teaching on others, there just weren't enough people who felt there was any point in making a stand. Especially when those in higher places they turned to for help told them there was no option but to let the place close. Cuts were coming in thick and fast from central Government and councils sat up, offered minimum resistance, then buckled.

Staff started to drift to other jobs or areas or just travelled on again. The centre did not 'justify further expenditure' and the buildings were 'badly (and suddenly) in need of radical and urgent repair.' The fire safety also became an issue - suddenly. In the end, they'd given in. Some had given it a go - but it had only been half-hearted.

It seemed longer ago than that. Ages. They had occupied for a while – and carried on the classes they could still run as volunteers at weekends and holidays – at least it made a change from the drudgery of the jobs that weren't being cut. Anna was taking the Drama Groups.

The Dance Routines had started it all; in fives and sixes in the Saturday morning, Drama Group showing off what they had learned in 'Music' the previous Saturday afternoon. It became a kind of a showcase: another opportunity for an audience for their efforts. Sometimes it was a song, sometimes a dance - the sequences getting more and more complicated as weeks passed.

The class told Anna about the music classes.

"It'd be better with music. He just gets us to say 1:2 and daft things 'til we get it right and then he puts the music on."

"And we have to close our eyes."

"...So we can think of ideas..."

"And pretend like we're dancing in our heads..."

"It's crap...".

"He can't dance…"

"…He's funny…"

"He can play all sorts…"

"Says he's got two left feet…"

"We've done Beethoven…"

"He was crap…"

"And we made an orchestra by clapping..."

"They were crap an' all..."

"The dancing's best…"

"…I think it's crap…"

"…I think he's a good teacher…"

"…Only 'cos you fancy him…"

"I do not!"

An idea showed itself.

When the morning was finished, Anna had her packed sandwiches and then left the Drama hut. It would be closed for the half term week. The site had once been a barracks - a few of the long, white, black-roofed huts were left, some had tables or benches inside for study groups while others were just used for floor space.

She passed the crèche's display - choked windows, the Handiwork shop and the smaller rooms used in the evenings for language classes and such, to where the Keep-fit, Judo and (now) Music was held.

Music (junior) was on.

She looked through the windows first, just a glance

to check that the people looked the right age and were doing the right things - and then stopped.

So that's who he was.

A few weeks earlier she had been hurrying to class and someone had held the gate open for her - unnecessarily as it always had to be pushed shut – and she'd been struck then by the beauty she saw now through the window. Overcome by unfamiliar shyness, she had just thanked him clumsily and gone to class, wishing she'd taken more care with her appearance that morning.

She had not seen him before or since – until now. She walked up the ramp and went into the room.

He had been watching the class go through a routine and was applauding when Anna came in to a chorus of bright, 'Hello Anna' and 'That's our acting teacher', 'It's called drama stupid', and 'Drama's crap an 'all' . He turned to greet her.

She was dazzled again.

He told them, a bit sharply perhaps, to sit down and be quiet which they ignored. Then he smiled at her in welcome and she forgot why she had come.

"You're Anna, I take it?" he smiled. "I'm Allan. Pleased to meet you. Come in."

"Thank you," now she remembered, "I've come about... um... I've had an idea about the music you do – and the drama they do with me – how about a Show?"

It sounded really stupid spoken out loud and where had all the words gone?

"Sounds marvellous. When do we start?" His smile was radiant.

"Shall I meet you after class to talk it over? Yes?" he suggested. "In the cafe across the road? We could talk about it and get something together..." She hoped she hadn't blushed at this, her mind was all over the place... or at least not as badly as she felt she had, or, at least, that he hadn't noticed.

"Sounds good, what time?" she managed.

Some quiet giggles brought another, sharper, "Quiet! Four?"

"Fine."

"See you then Anna. Glad you dropped in."

Another dazzling smile. She turned to walk out, horribly aware that he might be watching her and walking awkwardly as a result, aware that she had 'lost her cool' rather badly.

She had arrived late at the cafe, but he was later still, looking quite out of place in the grey, tacky surroundings.

"Been waiting long?"

"Not at all. Tea or coffee?"

"I haven't seen you there before," he said, after they'd given their orders. She didn't correct him. "How long have you been working there?"

She gave him a brief C.V. and then asked him the same question.

"I'm afraid I have a confession to make," he looked at her, sheepishly, "I don't."

"Don't what?"

Her mind raced.

"Work there," he said, "I was just calling on my flatmate - he works there."

"Ah! Oh well, we're here now."

"Are you doing anything tonight?"

She'd scored. He was gorgeous.

On the next date he had taken her to a concert, classical, and she'd enjoyed it. She loved theatres – the escape they offered from mediocre life. Allan had informed her about the music she was about to hear. She kept quiet about the fact it was one of her favourites. He didn't mean any harm by it. It was like that sometimes – the assumptions people made. Everybody assumes you like reggae and only reggae. It was nice to be with someone so enthusiastic and he was obviously trying to impress her – which was flattering.

He was critical of the orchestra after the concert had finished and he was walking with her to the bus stop. But it wasn't really their fault, he explained, being generous. He would have conducted it differently. That was his aim: he liked composing but to be a conductor was now his secret ambition! To put his own stamp on the music of the great and the dead. He made it sound as if they would be posthumously grateful. He'd invited her back to his house.

She had never been in a room quite so crowded with different kinds of musical instruments. She tried to find a space to sit on which wouldn't somehow serenade her descent.

"Sorry about that," said Allan, scooping up an armful of wood and string. "It's my flatmate, lazy sod, usually leaves his lunch on the couch so this isn't too bad. Like a drink?"

They spent the night together. He liked to be the one to direct proceedings, she noticed, didn't like too much innovation on her part – but very nice all the same. The following morning, the Sunday at the end of the half-term holiday, they slept late. They were awoken by Allan's bedroom door crashing open and a figure in denim and a t-shirt barging in. The figure grabbed up a guitar and swore.

"For fuck's sake Allan, was it too much to ask?"

The stranger strummed the guitar as he headed towards the door, hurriedly tuning it. "It's my bloody living, that's all!"

"Oh, sorry mate," Allan emerged sleepy eyed and looked at his watch. "I got a bit distracted."

Anna appeared, blinking in the morning light, from under the sheets.

"Morning?" she said.

The stranger turned, strummed the guitar then slammed his hand across the strings to halt the sound. The note hummed in the air. He grinned manically at Anna.

"Sorry about the language people! But I always expect the ugly bastard to be on his own!" He strummed again, turned and headed out of the door. They heard the front door shut on his way out.

"Who's that?" she asked.

"Ralph," said Allan, "my foul-mouthed slob of a flat mate."

"What was he so miffed about?"

"Oh he does busking, plays gigs - I was going to meet him and bring his violin or guitar along... he works nights - but you distracted me! Do you mind distracting me again!"

When the centre opened again, Anna went round to 'Music' again to share the idea about the 'Show'.

Calls of 'Hi Anna!' greeted her and she recognized the figure who was taking the class. He and some of the youngsters were trying to tap dance as she entered.

"Oh hello!" he said. "Anna? You're Anna! *The* Anna – they've told me loads about the stuff they do with you! Brilliant! Okay," he said to the class, "five minute break – try not to kill each other! Yeah," he turned back to Anne, "they act it all out. Has me in fits!"

"Same to you – you're the music teacher they keep going on about. Great! What do you think about...?"

"Doing a show? The kids told me! Brilliant idea – yeah! Why not?!"

"We could do drama, sketches, musical numbers... sell tickets?"

"Great – yeah – the Art lot could do the sets - the Sewing crew could do costumes..."

"And the woodwork lot could do the sets?"

From a small idea, it blossomed. Other groups were enthused and got involved. Parents dusted off old talents and took part. Rehearsal nights happened in the week and the centre was humming with activity again.

They planned a date 6 weeks away. The kids made up sketches, songs, practiced dances. Some were solos or duets – the comedians of the classes got their chance to shine. Anna was exhausted doing rehearsals as well as her cleaning job and dishwashing job – Ralph too went from his occasional night watch shifts, guarding empty offices, to pub work to rehearsals but it was fun - and that kept them going.

On the night, three children were sick, one parent who was on the programme to do two songs did four and had to be more or less forced off the stage and the audience, which included many of the performers who went up for their turn then back to watch the rest, clapped and cheered it all.

Waiting in the wings, one young lass turned to Anna excitedly as they waited for her cue and said, "I'm going to be an actress – I've decided!"

Anna watched her go onto the stage. She held the thin curtain in place so the audience wouldn't see into the wings too much. A blur of years seemed to pass her. 'I'm going to be an actress, I've decided' – how many now? Another curtain had hung in front of her then a heavy velvet one at her first rehearsal – ready. It seemed to be ready to be swept away by one sweep of her arm to admit her into the wonderful world of acting – but it still hung, heavy and unmoved, and now rather dusty, after all this time. A few bit parts here and there. This centre had been the best – working with kids and all the wonder of drama – and now this was to close. One temporary, mundane lousy job after another, never enough to live on. Her eyes prickled.

"Ey up, got anymore of that tape – the backdrop's threatening to give up and die – are you okay?" Ralph ducked under the curtain.

"Yeah, sure!"

"You sure? You look as if…"

"I'm fine!" she snapped.

"Okay! Okay!" He found the tape and bit off a chunk. "You don't sound very fine," he said around a mouthful of heavy duty tape.

"Sorry," she said, "I was just feeling… I dunno."

"Ah! The smell of the greasepaint is it? The call of the Theatre."

"That's right! The excitement – the first night nerves…"

"The second night cancellations…"

"The thrill of the audience…"

"The happy sound of heckling…"

"The magic of theatre…"

"The lousy plays? The mad directors? The sleeping audiences?"

"Oh shut up! If I want to feel sorry for myself…"

"Okay – sorry to interrupt!" He grinned at her and ducked under the improvised curtain of stitched together sheets to go and fix the scenery.

The night was a success. They had all had a magical time. Some of the older ones had worked on a short play with Anna and it had worked well. She'd done a monologue, one by Allan Bennet, which she loved. Ralph had done a violin and guitar duet with a younger musician who just needed a bit of encouragement. Allan had amazed them all with a piece on the centre's piano and bowed to the applause with a modest smile, five or six times, before being ushered off stage with assurances that, no, it hadn't been 'too high' for them.

The kids were euphoric with what they had achieved. The centre was crowded with Roman soldiers, pixies, clowns' hats and baking foil silver gowns; kids shouted bits of Shakespeare and snatches of song as they were collected by their various adults spilled out into the night and the walk home.

Then notice had come around that the Centre would not be re-opening, not even at weekends as cuts had had to be implemented. It was likely the land would be sold off.

They had never been well organised and the resistance was patchy and half-hearted. Contracts had been finished anyway and would not be renewed, they were told. People didn't want to spoil their chances elsewhere - wherever 'elsewhere' was. A petition was sent round, signed and sent in to be filed alongside every other petition, in alphabetical order, into the bin. When a few had continued to hold classes, children had been kept away.

"We want to do this in a law-abiding way, see?"

They had argued that there wasn't one because all effective ways were now illegal, but they hadn't been invited back, nor offered a second cup of tea.

"They don't like the idea. Yours?"

"The same."

"That's it then. No parking on a yellow line. Even when they've painted it on the wheels of your car."

"Have we done this street?"

"No. Last one. Shall we bother?"

"Why not? It just might be the stronghold of militancy."

It wasn't.

Anna and Ralph had to admit defeat - in the battle if not the war.

Fewer people turned up to class or to organise as the days passed. There didn't seem to be an alternative to giving up. By the time they came to Officially Close the place there was only a small line of people by the main gate not across it - with a few placards stating protest and what they wanted: the Centre left as a Centre.

'They' drove in past them, changed the locks, put up some signs about trespassers and drove out again. The placard carriers went home to consolation prizes of tea and hot chocolate and wry remarks on the whole business.

"Looks like we're back on Maggie's Farm again."

It had been a good time. It was good to use their skills. Now they had to pack up their skills and put them away. Ralph went back to his night watch work and pulling pints and busking; Anna to her various bits of work.

Anna went around to see Allan, who was writing.

"A walkover that's what it was... a fiasco..."

"Hm? Was it? Sorry I missed it. These exams."

"...A picnic, a circus, and all clowns..."

"Did they get through then?"

"You could say that."

"You and Ralph going around on the knocker again?"

"No point. Got nowhere first time. It's over. Picket line? They probably thought we were a bus-queue!"

"Don't touch that."

"For your exam?"

"Yes."

"So I'll get down to the office and sign on again."

"Hm."

"And that's it."

"S'pose so."

"It's a real shame."

"After all that."

"Hmm."

"If only we'd been better prepared - more organised from the start."

"Hmm."

"I hardly knew any of the people there until we had the Show. If only we had..."

"Yes."

"I can see you're fascinated."

"Yes."

"Good job I won the pools this morning or I would be in shit-creek."

"Hmm."

"Thanks for your support, Tiger."

She left.

"Hmm. Anna…?"

In the kitchen, by 9pm, the end of her shift, Anna's back and calves were aching despite the discreet exercises she'd been doing while reminiscing.

The restaurant had closed and the others had gone but there were still some bits to do and the wiping round to leave it clear for the morning. She stacked the last of the banana-split glasses - always the most difficult to get clean - and wrung out a hot cloth.

When she had finished, she had a quick look in the fridge to see if there was anything 'disappear-able'. She was ravenous - but, too late, it was locked for the night and Jones had the key.

"MISS Hanley! What are you doing?"

Anna nearly jumped out of her skin.

"Reny! You scared me to death!"

"Like a midnight snack?" Reny waved aloft a plastic bag. "Courtesy of the Chef. And me of course," he bowed, modestly.

"When did you get that out?"

"Mo reminded me before he locked it."

"Mo!?"

"I've got a system - Mo doesn't mind - not too much and not too often and keep switching what you

118

take. They never miss it. I've promised him never to touch the blue cheese because he's soft on that... So..." he held up the bag, "it's a French bread, pate and fruit gateaux supper for me! Again! Care to join me? Real butter too!"

Reny hadn't been working there long but he seemed to have got the hang of how to survive pretty quickly. He had had to leave home suddenly some weeks ago and had been looking for somewhere else to live. Anna had told him about Liz's place across the street from her and Allan's place.

They left together. The bar-side was still open and its light fell across the rows of cars lined up in the carpark. Anna and Reny's shadows flickered red to blue and over grey shapes as they headed through the car park towards home, the voices from the bar fading behind them.

At the far side, in the shadow of some bushes, a voice was muttering - it sounded almost like swearing. They looked around to locate the drunk.

It was coming from under a raised bonnet from which trousered hips and legs hung to the ground while the top half of the body was lost in the metal maw. It looked as if the car had just stopped chewing its victim to let them pass.

"Are you stuck?"

"What? Ow!"

The victim straightened up in fright, hit the bonnet and emerged from under it, rubbing his head. A silhouette under the bush's shadow.

"I can't tell what the matter is - it just won't start."

"Have you driven much today?" Reny asked authoritatively.

"No, not at all, why?"

"It's been damp all day, and the frost's early tonight - it could be your plugs."

The silhouette didn't respond to this information nor seem to be particularly enlightened by it.

"Here, I'll have a look. Got any light?"

Anna produced a light-up key-ring,

"And if you open one of the doors the inside light will come on - that'd help."

"Of course," said Arthur, and hurried to open one. "This is very nice of you, jolly decent, I was going to call a garage but...'

He stopped as he came around to the front again and saw Reny's war plumage glowing in the torchlight above the engine.

"....Oh," said Arthur, in a shock of recognition.

"Won't be a minute."

Reny's arms were deep in machinery.

"There you go. Now try that."

Arthur did. The engine grunted with surprise and awoke.

"Why, thank you very much, young man."

Arthur hesitated for a shudder of time then extended a hand and shook Reny's hand warmly, his eyes warily on the war-plume.

"No problem. I like doing cars."

"Thank you!" Arthur nodded at Anna. She seemed nice too, even though she was ...er...he nodded goodnight.

They moved on after the big Jag had reversed out and driven off into the night.

"Funny fellah, that. I'm sure he was hanging around our place early on, frightening everybody. Thought he was the filth when I first saw him."

Chapter 12

Reny lived in the basement of the house opposite Anna's. He tended to keep to his own company, according to Liz. He was quite a bit younger than the others there. They went down the stone steps by the side of the front door, carpeted with a thickness of rotting leaves, to where the servants' entrance had been.

Inside, Reny lit a small candle which was stuck in a familiar looking pale-blue saucer. The yellow light wavered over the grey concrete floor and walls. There was what looked like a back seat from a bus, resting on its springs. The bed seemed to be a long heap of old clothes, blankets and bits of cloth. A large box on its side doubled as a chair and a cocktail cabinet. Familiar looking bottles of beer lurked within.

Reny went around lighting more candles, small red, ornate ones - rather like the ones you might find in a restaurant. Anna shivered. The air was heavy with damp and the cold swept in with every breath. Reny lit a small paraffin stove that gave out a gesture of heat with wafts of fumes.

"I need to get it fixed up better than this," Reny

was saying, unwrapping their supper. "I think the last lot who lived here took everything with them."

"There'd be some stuff upstairs you could have. And you can come and look round ours for anything you need. There were eight of us there... it takes ages on your own. I'm going to get some more people in, actually, you could just move across. Why not? Or move upstairs. Liz is alright."

"Thanks. But I haven't had a place of my own before. To myself. I want to do this room up. Have it as my own. I reckon it could be good. Paint it. Get a decent fire from somewhere..."

"By yourself?" It wasn't the cosiest place to be on your own.

"Well, not for long, I hope. But we'll have to see what happens."

"What's likely to happen?"

Reny hesitated.

"A friend of mine might be coming down soon. Mike. Well, more than likely actually. He's probably going to get thrown out. Probably."

"Of what?"

"His home. That's what happened to me. When they found out. I don't care though. They can stuff it!" He was suddenly angry.

He was quiet for a minute. "Not very nice though. Suddenly, they don't even like you. The' loving family'. Talk about 'pretend family'. But they can go to hell."

She could hear the choke in his voice, stifled in anger.

"What's happening with Mike?"

"He's set on telling his dad. About us. His mum's already guessed. She went to the church for guidance! Can you believe it? I was brought up to love my neighbour - but the fact that I do just that threw them into complete confusion! I don't know what they told her - probably to have us exorcised and the house de-fumigated! He's going to break it to his dad sometime this week. He didn't want me to be there, just in case. I said he should write but that's not his way. Not Mike." Reny smiled, "His mum and dad and me used to get on great. But only because they didn't know. My dad... I thought he was going to kill me. If I'd told him I'd murdered a baby, he wouldn't have thought it half so bad. A sod, isn't it?"

Anna agreed. It was a sod.

"At least you got out. A lot don't."

"I know. As long as Mike gets here, we'll be alright. Fix this place up, s'all I want, try and find him a job. I can't go home again now. But I don't care. You'd like Mike. You'd get on. Are you going to be living here long?"

"As long as they'll let me. We'll have to see. Bring him round when he gets here - we'll have a welcoming party."

"Sound!"

Reny tore up the bread and cut the pate with restaurant knives. They had a candle-lit picnic on blue plates amidst the liquid shadows. Anna wouldn't have liked to have been there on her own in the jagged shadow under the stairs.

"That's where The Creature lives," said Reny. "Would you like to meet him?"

"No ta."

"Look what I've got!" he held up a tiny packet wrapped in cellophane. "Present from Liz. Leading me astray she is. Thank god... like some?"

Anna contributed papers and tobacco and Reny rolled it up - inexpertly.

They sat on the bizarre collection of furniture and smoked and talked.

"What time is it?" said Anna, eventually. "I said I'd meet Ralph to go postering when he finished work."

"In the middle of the night? It's 11.30."

"Best time. Work again tomorrow."

"What's it for?"

"The rally."

"Can I come?"

"Yeah. Do. You can be look-out."

"Sounds exciting!"

They both had to struggle to get their trainers back on through an unfamiliar fug of smoke induced ineptitude.

"Could be very exciting since I can't see further than about ten feet."

"That's better than either of us any way. We just run from anything that moves. Last time we hardly got any posters up and ran about twenty miles."

Anna had managed to get her boots back on and

was now tracking down the ends of the laces ponderously. She'd never noticed before how the tiny little stripes spiralled around them so prettily. They seemed unusually lively as she struggled doggedly to get them to tie. Every sensation of the cold cement floor, the hard-outer rim and soft, familiar interiors of each shoe, the tightening across the top of each foot as she pulled the burning laces - were all infinitely fascinating. She seemed to have spent half the night just putting her trainers on. Reny seemed to be having the same difficulty with the fingers of his gloves.

"What time is it?"

"11.40!"

They walked a thousand long miles uphill to the bus stop. The lights of the town were bright and colourful like a huge fairground all for free. The double-decker death wagon with all the long faces and staring eyes trundling through the night forever was a huge joke, put on especially for them and not real at all. Were they supposed to take this seriously - these prison walls?

Reny, determined to stay cool, put on a super-serious I'm not really stoned-out-of-my-box expression. It was just that everybody else on the whole bus was wearing exactly the same expression.

Reny and Anna tried to avoid each other's eye but the carefully constructed dam of self-control and composure gradually erupted and shattered; their faces collapsed first, clenched tight to hold the laughter in until their throats hurt and eyes watered, but it was too late and a tiny sound of a laugh from one of them found the breach. The whole structure collapsed and they laughed out loud - the disapproving looks from the other passengers only fuelled the fire and oiled the madness until they wanted, needed, to stop laughing but couldn't, their faces red, eyes running and breath hurting.

"Good stuff this. Knocks hell out of lager," was Reny's comment that set them off again.

They floundered off at the right stop, still giggling at the baleful faces they left behind.

Ralph, tired already from the night's work, recognised their condition at about fifty yards. They made a special effort in his honour but fumbling about with the packet of paste in the public toilet and mixing it with the stick which kept slipping out of their hands as they took turns and having to be rescued from the slimy mess and being watched throughout by a highly intrigued tramp who was resting out of the cold on the floor - all seemed hilarious.

Then it was out into the night and fighting with great sheets of gluey paper which flapped, grew, expanded in all directions and fought back valiantly - as any brave poster should - against their efforts to stick them onto walls, while the glue got in their hair, their eyes and up their noses. Ralph didn't seem to enter into the spirit of things at all and kept looking round for police like someone in a Carry On. Reny took turns at lookout and gave the alarm when an off-duty ice-cream van went past which sent them running for cover and laughing again but just annoyed Ralph who'd had a hard day.

They covered the sub-way, the supermarket

entrance, some Nazi-graffiti and under a fly-over. Ralph wasn't getting much help - with them fooling around, giggling and flicking glue - and it made him feel about a thousand years old. A car appeared out of the night and slid past them. Ralph found himself looking into the blue eyes of the uniformed passenger as he rode by. Ralph was in the middle of re-loading the brush and froze, thinking of the fine he could get but couldn't pay.

"You're supposed to be keeping an eye-out!"

Reny and Anna leapt about, looking frantically everywhere for miniature police-cars.

Ralph stuck the poster up, grabbed the bucket, the rolls of posters and pushed the other two with him down a side-street before the car could get back around the one-way system and start the 'ello'ello'ello' routine.

Reny and Anna sobered up a bit but it didn't last long. Another time, Ralph was just about to attack an inviting length of hoarding in a prime place for high visibility when he realised the car parked nearby had a red-stripe round it and two silent shadows sitting in it. Reny wanted to go and turn it over but was persuaded that this wasn't the right time for that.

Ralph walked on ahead of the other two who were arm in arm, apparently swapping whispered confidences. He wished he was somewhere else. Or that they were. He had never realized it before but he didn't like Reny.

There was a monument to something in a mini-park full of empty flower beds.

"We'll put one here," said Ralph.

"But that's a war memorial!" Reny stated, as if he was addressing a board meeting and they were off again laughing and repeating the statement as pompously as they could, 'But that's a war-memorial!'

"They'd understand," muttered Ralph, sticking up the last poster. "What were they fighting for anyway but a better world?"

He heard something and turned. At the entrance to the park was a figure in uniform and they could hear the crackle as he talked into his radio.

"Move!"

They ran and walked back the other way, out of the park and back under the overpass. The police car had to go around the one-way system, then it turned and headed their way, driving past all the posters they had put up there.

"Down here," said Ralph.

They turned and Ralph led the way down the main road.

"Get ready to go for it at the next turn!"

They reached it and- broke into an all-out sprint. Leading, Ralph dodged down a side-alley, out the other end, over a low wall, across a grass space and over to a bus shelter where they came to a stop, gasping for breath. A van full of navy blue went past but it didn't stop.

"Another fine saved! We'll be rich if we keep doing that."

They got their breath back, checked all was clear and headed home.

"Thanks for all your help," said Ralph.

"I held the bucket!" Anna said, defensively.

"Great, the pavement could have done that."

"I ran as fast as you!"

"Tough shit if you hadn't - I wouldn't have come to rescue you."

"No, but you'd have rescued the bucket."

"True, buckets cost, Friends are free."

"How would you know?"

"Free to leave. So they do. So I hang onto my buckets."

"Are you coming back to my place?" asked Reny when they'd reached the Court. "For a snack?" For some reason, he was hungry again.

"Come to ours," said Anna. "We've got cornflakes!"

"How's your place over there?" asked Ralph, making an effort. "You in the basement?"

"Yeah. S'great. Better than a penthouse - why look down chimney-pots when you can see up trouser legs? That set them off again." Ralph managed a rueful smile.

When they got upstairs there was a light already on in the living-room and a figure waiting on the rug-covered settee who raised her head and looked at them out of-tear-reddened eyes.

"I wondered where you were," it said, in a little voice, looking at Ralph.

Anna took one look and said, "I'll take you up on

that offer of a sandwich after all, Ren."

She took Reny's arm and guided him, rather firmly, out of the door and back down the stairs. She left Ralph where he was, looking at the figure and completely unaware of Reny and Anna leaving - or bursting into flames or levitating round the room if they had done either of those things.

"Where are we going?" asked Reny, halfway down the stairs.

"Away," explained Anna.

"Who was that on the couch?"

"I'll introduce you when you need a bad time, OK?"

"Does Ralph know her?"

"He thinks so."

"You don't like her?"

"I love her, that's why we're running down these stairs."

"Hard to get, eh? Never works, mind. Take it from me."

They got back to Reny's 'penthouse' and finished off the French bread and pate with a bad attack of the munchies and did battle with the rummage sale of a bed. Reny re-lit the heater to leave it burning all night between some old bricks to make sure it stayed upright. They sorted out enough blankets to cover them both. Reny didn't help for long. Anna tucked some coats around the sleeping figure and herself. His face looked very thin, and too young for its five-o'clock shadow, with the mad banner falling over the pillow. She blew out the last of the candles and they snuggled close and warm, stoned and oblivious.

Lying down, Anna saw that the full moon had risen and was sending silver rays through the basement window as bright as if from a lighthouse, grown tired of blinking.

It was good to have a night-light to keep the shadows away.

*

The decisions to invest in machinery and work now seemed a poor one. Each producer could not get enough return on all the money poured in before a competitor with newer machinery swept the board. Too much money tied up in machinery - that was fast becoming obsolete as new models leapt ahead, producing more and faster. Yesterday's profit rates were no more. The maximum amount of money had been invested – too late. The whole system reached the top of the cycle again and began to lurch, by increments, back into recession.

Chapter 13

Across the street, after his initial shock at seeing her suddenly appear as if out of nowhere in the middle of the night, and wanting desperately to be able to follow the intelligent line of action and send her home straightaway in a taxi, Ralph had ended up sitting on the couch with an arm round her, listening.

Angie's life was in ruins. And the man she loved so much and who meant so much to her had gone off with someone else. Again. After telling her she was 'useless' and no partner for anyone who was going anywhere in the world etc. etc. Nothing new. And after the brief flurry of rebellious thoughts, Ralph's mind settled back into a pattern of established behaviour.

It wasn't too much to ask was it, after all? Someone to talk to who'd listen. He'd heard a lot of it before and versions of the rest but how could he deny her after all she'd been through in her short, crisis-ridden life? She had always been so vulnerable. From the very first time he'd met her...

It had been in the worst time of year when making the effort to enjoy yourself had become too much hard work, when the festive cheer had overwhelmed and nauseated everything in its path until finally it had caved in on itself, leaving a trough where battered paper-cups and torn-streamers settled and the old year drained away.

Ralph was musing over its dregs, together with those of the night's treat-pint, and wondering if it was worth going through the same again of either. All it seemed to do was lend an illusion and leave a pain, steal your wallet with one hand and your time with another.

He was getting maudling. It was alright for him to sit there and feel sorry for himself - there were others who just had to get on with it, with worse worries and who had other people depending on them.

But that only made it even worse - feeling totally miserable, as well as guilty about feeling totally miserable. At least other people, in a worse situation, could feel justified in being depressed. He didn't even have that comfort.

But at least he only had himself to worry about. Although only himself to do the worrying. There was nobody else who would give a monkey's if he fell off the nearest bridge.

It hadn't been a bad morning out after all, busking with the violin. People seemed to give more if they saw you out in the freezing cold which was stupid because you can't eat sunshine.

He always seemed to time it right - get trained as a draughtsman just as the market was glutted with people trained in the same skill and just as all the firms needing those skills were going bust.

Then he'd finally got on the music course he had always wanted to do - just as the decision had been made somewhere to cut Arts Grants and close theatres and orchestras. They probably had all the musicians they wanted for the time being and he was surplus to requirements.

Maybe, after all, there was too much music in the world?

Normally he would have been out with Laura now but that had all finished.

Time passes.

People change and grow.

Apart.

He missed her.

Sharing a house with Allan was rapidly becoming unbearable but there didn't seem to be any alternative just yet.

Things really were looking up.

Then someone sat down in the seat opposite. He hadn't seen her in here before although it was his local. She looked as if she had been crying, very recently. She sipped at her drink and glowered at the world.

"You OK?" He was trying to place where he'd seen that red-tinted hair before. And those eyes.

They glanced over his attire and turned their attention to something more worthy of their gaze. Like the ash-tray on the next table. Snotty!

But then he looked at it from her point of view: some horrible, leery bloke trying to make a pick–up.

He wished Anna or Laura was there to make things easier.

Then he remembered.

"I think you live near me - Nelson Street?"

"That's right!" surprise wrenched a response and acknowledgement of his existence but the mistake was soon realised and communication shut down again as she turned, very pointedly, away.

"I'm at 25..." he continued, thinking what a brilliantly enthralling piece of news that was and why didn't he just go home and stick his head in the sink?

"Well I hope everything's alright," he blundered on. "You do look upset, I just wondered," Ralph got up to leave, draining his pint glass and picking up his violin case.

"Oh! You the musician then?"

THE musician? That sounded nice! And he existed again - she was actually looking at him!

"Well not the only one, but probably the best, yes!"

An actual smile. The sun had come out when all had seemed rain.

"You're professional, aren't you?" The tone had almost half-decided to be slightly interested. He could not, did not resist. He could not disappoint those eyes with the truth.

At least not with all of it.

"Oh yes," he casually said. Professional means you earn money from whatever it is – which he did!

And there it was again - a spark of interest in the smoke.

Feed it.

"Not for long though, I'm not quite at the top yet. Bit to go yet." Well that was true at any rate. He certainly had quite a bit to go. "But I'm developing my own style, enjoying myself, doing different things..." That was so true it was an understatement.

She looked really interested.

"You do music? You like music?" he said. A fellow traveller, a fellow soul?

She almost shrugged in her answer but conveyed her meaning without having to do anything so gross.

"Sure. It's nice."

Ralph boggled a bit at that and wondered where to go from there.

She continued, "We hear you sometimes when we go past your house. My... a friend of mine... thinks you're really good."

Ralph suddenly felt better - a lot better than he had been feeling for a while. It was the nicest thing anyone had told him since he'd heard the Facts of Life.

"Nice to be appreciated. Usually I just get complaints."

"Yes, so do we. With the parties. We've got one on tonight actually..." this faded and she looked sad, and something like angry as well. Ralph had a quick look round, wondering where the reckless revellers were hiding or when they were due to arrive. Had no-one turned up? Or had it been a tea-party and they had already gone home? She didn't look the tea-party-type. She could see the question on his face.

"They're back at the house. I needed some air."

Ralph realised he was still standing, holding his glass and his case. He didn't know what else to say. She obviously needed some time to herself to sort something out that had nothing to do with him. And she wasn't in the last stages of depression after all. And they'd talk again sometime.

Then, suddenly, out of the blue-grey of the rest of the weekend, came the promise, the magic phrase to blow all the blues away – the incantation to the bandits' treasure

"Would you like to come to my party?" Pardon? Had he heard right?

"I know it's late and a bit short notice but you could pop home and change - there are quite a few arty-types there, but no musicians. It's a party for my birthday and my... a friend's just got his first contract with a firm, so..." she stood up, leaving her drink and picked up her bag, smiling at him.

'This sounds a bit strange,' suggested Ralph's mind, 'something funny about all this.' But he wasn't listening.

"If you just go home and change, I'll wait. Won't take a minute."

"Sure!" he blinked. Change? What into? But they'd reached the door and she was smiling at him and waiting for him to open it. So he forgot to ask.

They reached No. 25 and he led her in through the

front door. The living room was decent, thank God - the slob hadn't left his lunch on the couch. Ralph shifted a cornet, moved a set of tom-toms and invited Angela, that was her name, to 'make herself at home while he slipped into something more comfortable', which earned him another one of those smiles.

His mind had been ransacking his wardrobe - or, rather, his unique collection of coat hangers - since they'd left the pub. There was nothing that would meet the present requirement. He had never had to put on clothes to enjoy himself before. The opposite, yes, he had got the hang of that quite quickly, but this was a new idea and found him ill-prepared. He went straight to Allan's room. He was out with Anna. There was a full-length mirror in the door of the bulging wardrobe. Ralph got busy.

When he came back downstairs dressed in Allan's finest, Angela looked pleased (relieved?) with the results of his efforts. And still beautiful. What had she been crying about earlier? They left for the party.

Ralph had been expecting... what he hadn't been expecting was a house full of people and a party in full, if not swing, then full hum.

People really were dressed up. Angela, in a white dress he hadn't noticed under her coat, put them all in the shade but they were all doing their best. He didn't look too bad himself; he had to admit, catching sight of his strange reflection. Angela put her arm through his, friendly like, as they went in, and kept it there as they moved through the milling crowd to the drinks table - heavily laden, he was pleased to see.

'Hello's' came from all sides and, "Angel, darling,

we thought you'd gone forever, come over here, don't keep him to yourself."

Angie kept introducing him to a dazzling array of outfits with beautiful people inside them and then leading him on to more introductions. He felt like the centre of attention and kept a firm hold on the treble scotch he'd poured for moral support. It was amazing what an effect could be had by a covering of well-designed fabric.

"This is Ralph Pederson," Angie was saying again. "You know?"

There was a little uncertainty here on the faces of people who were used to trying to recall the significance of a name when meeting the person attached to it, but Angie would murmur 'musician' as a hint and they'd cotton-on immediately and welcome him like a long-lost lover. Ralph didn't mind a bit. He smiled into smiling eyes and felt pretty good. He could do this forever.

They never hung around to develop a conversation of any kind, Angie would lead him on to another group or couple or hopeful individual, but everyone there seemed to be following the same pattern and the air pinged with introductions, greetings and names ringing bells.

They found a space. Ralph was looking around to see how to turn the music up. Angela was looking around.

"This your flat?"

"Yes, all mine. How long have you had that house? Been there long?"

"Not long."

He wouldn't explain about the shared digs and the rent arrears just at that moment.

"Lived here long?" If he could get her talking, he could postpone his own revelations a bit longer and stay in range of that smile.

"Not really."

She was looking past him at something in the other room and then said, "Like to dance?" She took his free hand and smiled up at him. He put down the whisky and followed her through to an area where people were moving about in time to a song that was just finishing. Angela didn't seem to mind that the music was over and stood close, holding him and swaying slightly, in perfect time to the silence, until someone changed the record.

The next one seemed to demand a more energetic response but that didn't matter either and they moved around the tiny circle of stripped pine, slow and close. People seemed to be noticing them - she was probably used to that - or was he just feeling paranoid?

A slow dance to a fast record. Angie resting her head on his shoulder. She was wearing perfume, a rich, subtle scent. She looked at him to check he was happy and he managed to smile back.

She certainly seemed to have taken a shine to him all of a sudden between here and the pub but he didn't want to consider possible reasons. He was glad, that was all.

Even here in her own place there was something strangely vulnerable about her. She was so little, elegant - dainty? Maybe 'precious' was the word, said his mind, but that was unkind so he hung onto 'vulnerable'. She looked happy enough now and whatever had happened to upset her seemed to be forgotten. Though he was glad it had happened.

She said she didn't like the next record and they moved off the dance-floor. Ralph decided to play 'the mysterious stranger' to the rest of the party. He knew now why he had had to change - it was important here to be the right sort of person and even more important to look the right sort of person. A smooth glamour was here of hair and nails that shone and clothes that were cut just right in a shallow light overall of a mellow topiary.

He realised that someone was looking at him and trying to catch his eye, then a lightweight suit blocked the view and the level of conversation immediately around him seemed to drop a few decibels.

"Ralph Pederson," whoever it was had found his name out, anyway, "...Tom...Tom Hart. Pleased to meet you."

The executive type introduced himself. Ralph shook the proffered hand and wondered who the hell this was.

Angela had been leading the way to the kitchen but now she had turned and come back to slip her arm through Ralph's.

"You're in the musical world, I gather. I'm afraid your name is new to me. You must excuse my ignorance," said Tom.

"That's okay," Ralph forgave him, generously, and smiled.

Tom looked taken aback at this and adjusted his stance. Ralph felt he was being strafed with ego and aggro in equal quantities. The guy was doing the whole bit; the level stare, straight mouth, full-frontal posture. Perhaps he'd been taking lessons in 'How To Scare The Pants Off People At Parties'? Ralph waited to see what had come next on the course.

Tom floundered for a minute then said, "I'd be interested to hear your work - any friend of Angela's is a friend of mine." (The penny dropped this time and Ralph realised that he was playing piggy-in-the-middle, only no one had told him.)

"Are you in Town at the moment?" Tom asked, persistently.

He pronounced 'town' the way Allan did when he was trying to impress - 'Tyne'. It was just as well Ralph had heard it before and knew he wasn't referring to a northern river or he would have been totally confused.

As it was, he didn't hesitate. "The Royale," he said, one of his favourite pitches, "you must drop by."

Mix that in your cocktail and swallow it, you yuppie git.

"The Royale, Covent Garden?" Tom's face was a picture of fluster. He looked Ralph up and down, taking in the designer suit. It was just as well he didn't have x-ray eyes as Ralph's undies were all his own.

Ralph looked at Tom as if with renewed interest, "There's another?" he asked, innocently. Tom blinked and took a sip of his drink. Ralph picked up a glass, poured out another whisky and raised it in a toast.

"A good Season?" He wasn't sure if that was the sort of thing a professional violinist would drink to and suspected it wasn't - but it was the best he could think of in the circumstances. He took a swallow and decided that allowing the enemy a dignified retreat would be a wise tactic given that all his own ammunition consisted of blank cartridges and someone else's camouflage.

"You live here as well then?" he asked, innocent again.

Tom looked at Angie for the first time at this question. Neither looked enthralled with the other.

"No, just a guest. An old friend, you might say."

"Where's your other friend?" said Angela suddenly.

They exchanged the briefest of veiled, polite glowers then Tom looked back at Ralph who'd been watching the fun over the rim of his glass.

"She left, I think. But speaking for myself, I don't keep tabs on my friends."

"Maybe you should," she murmured, with the sweetest of smiles, and with a slight tug she asked Ralph to move away with her and he complied, raising his glass again to Tom on the way past but not receiving any more jovial response than a well-practiced death-stare. Oh dear, it looked like Fido's hackles were up.

Ralph re-filled his glass. So he was being used to grout over cracks in someone else's relationship, but at least he could come out of it with a decent hangover. He might have guessed someone like Angie wouldn't take a sudden shine to someone like him without some ulterior motive. He had just met the motive and it was more ulterior than he might have expected.

They reached the kitchen and Angie turned to him and smiled again. He liked her less. He should have guessed there was something funny going on. But she was looking at him differently. Or was it the whisky?

"I didn't know you were at the Garden? You didn't tell me that. Were you making it up?"

"No, why should I?" He liked his lie. He would not betray it. The whisky urged him on.

"What else haven't you told me?" She leaned closer, looking up at him.

Why this, when the audience was out of view in the other room, still pouring oil on troubled fire? Maybe he did like her as much as he'd first imagined after all?

"Would you believe I'm an undercover agent and that my father was an African prince?"

"You were making it up!" She drew back again.

"No - but he might have been Welsh!" She didn't laugh.

"No honestly, that part was true - why don't you believe me? What about you? I know nothing at all about you except you throw good parties, think music's 'nice' and keep giving me whisky..." He paused. "Not much else I need to know really." She kissed him.

Ralph glanced round quickly expecting the first punch to arrive but there was no one there and the ulterior was still out of sight. She really had kissed him.

God, she was lovely. Or was it the whisky?

"Are you really at the Royale?" She was flirting with him now.

Did it really matter that much?

"Why don't you come and see for yourself?"

He badly wanted to kiss her again, for longer. For ages longer.

She considered this.

"Alright. But would I be able to see you? In the orchestra?"

"I'll stand up and yell 'Hey, Angie!' half way through the quiet bit, yeah? No, it won't be a problem... I'm on solo, remember?"

What was he getting himself into?

"Anyway, what are you into?"

Or what do you want me to think you are into? As if I care!

"Interiors."

"You're a surgeon?"

She laughed.

"Design, silly, advertising. Contract for six months. Some clients are here tonight actually. Or they were. I want my own business one day, producing my own ideas and working for myself... One day soon."

"Good luck." And I want my own orchestra. One day soon.

"How did you get into doing that?"

The cosy chat in the kitchen meandered on aimlessly enough around music and its working world, contracts and design and deadlines, sponsors and deals. Angela pointed out the draped material and use of lights in the other room, "You can't see it very well with all the people here, but it looks good. Those lampshades are my design. What d'ye think?"

Ralph felt worse as the night soothed into morning - and it wasn't just the whisky. Alright, he'd wanted to hold his own when under flak from the up-and-coming-young, successful, well-off-pain-in-the-ass but Angie was alright really. A bit unsure of herself, seemed to need approval too much, vulnerable. And another word but he couldn't think of it. What would happen to her if, or when, 'one day soon' did a bunk over the nearest horizon - with its swag bag full of youth as it usually did?

Meanwhile, along comes Mr Wonderful in his mate's suit and starts telling lies about his brilliant career as a successful concert violinist just to hold her attention.

One woman - who'd been making eyes at Ralph earlier on came through and whispered something to Angie, eyeing Ralph at the same time. He caught the odd word and the name 'Tom' but Angie's response was, "I couldn't care less. Good riddance!"

The messenger's face registered disappointment at this and she went out, giving Ralph the benefit of another searing unspoken promise - or threat - he couldn't decide which, as she passed.

"So," Angie brightened, "am I invited to the

Theatre?"

"I'd like to see you there."

"When?"

"Tomorrow? Eight o'clock?"

"Could I get a ticket? It'll be booked up?"

"Don't worry about a ticket, I'll arrange it so you don't need one."

That much should be easy enough.

"You be coming alone?" It would be worse if she brought someone.

"Will I be safe alone?"

"Ought to be. But bring earplugs in case."

She laughed. Exquisite had been the word he had been looking for.

"I'll be by the door when you arrive."

That was also very true - if just a little misleading.

"I love music," she said, without a shrug. "Don't you ever get nervous in front of all those crowds?"

He left before the party ended and went home feeling like he'd just found a twenty-quid note in his jeans

When he awoke, sober, that afternoon, and remembered, it was as if he had just shredded the same note in the launderette. The night before and what he had said and what he had arranged all came to visit him in the light of day and he wanted to crawl back under the heavy blankets and die, pretend it had never happened and that he had never, really, been born.

But the world demanded payment and 7:30 found him outside the 'Royale', warming the violin and the night with a comforting soiree as people hurried by to witness the more comfortable versions inside.

The violin always went down better than the guitar here and he chose his favourite piece of music and got lost in it. Tonight was special so the case remained closed at his feet. He didn't want pennies tonight. There was no room for him on the inside but that applied to many others and he played for them all. One coin sang on the pavement but he resisted the urge to pick it up and fling it back.

Passers-by hesitated, paused, and gradually a small group formed and grew. Eyes closed, he didn't see them but he knew they were there.

There was stillness inside the half-circle which muffled the sound of walkers outside and the hum of traffic beyond. The stone walls trapped the music and threw it down again to the ring of faces while dusk gathered, rain threatened as the little group listened quietly on the cobbles among the grey-white pillars and crowd-worn steps.

When he looked up to acknowledge the applause, he saw her. She had already turned away and was walking back the way she must have come. She didn't look back. So... he let her go.

Then he smiled at the crowd to thank them for their applause and bowed. He opened the old case after all - so he didn't sell tickets? What was the difference? People looked happy and were generous and moved on, looking back at him.

She was halfway back to the far corner of the

square by the time he caught up with her.

"Alright, I'm sorry - but I thought you'd laugh," he said, trying to get his breath back. He made a mental note to do something about his deplorable state of fitness.

"And what on earth made you think that?"

She was dressed as some people do for a night at the theatre.

"Well this is Covent Garden, the Royale, I am playing solo, you didn't need a ticket and... I am a professional," he shook the cloth-bag that held his earnings to prove it.

"You're just another liar! Leave me alone!"

"Hey, you could just laugh, tell me I'm a jerk - as if I didn't know - and then we could go and have a pizza on my earnings - one each even! You must admit I can play the thing!"

She didn't answer this but at least she'd slowed down. But it had gone sour. He had known it would when he'd woken up that morning. Best not to take it any further.

"OK, nice to have met you and all that. Sorry you reckon I'm a shit. It wasn't meant like that but I expect you're right. See you. And sorry." He turned and started back to the theatre. She stopped and watched him walk away. He stopped on the kerb before crossing back over - and glanced back.

He walked back to her.

"And one day I'll be on the inside and you won't hear me for free - so you could say I was just anticipating a bit, sort of, nostalgia in reverse."

A small reluctant smile flickered, but was quickly doused.

"I suppose you were hoping to make a fool of me in front of everyone?"

Ralph glanced round at the hurrying, uncaring crowds.

"Everybody at home, I mean. They all think you're this great violin-player and you're... you're a beggar!"

Ralph's professional pride was cut to the quick.

"A busker, actually! And who's 'everybody'? That lot at the party? I couldn't give a monkey's if that lot thought I was a mass murderer - in fact I'd like that because then they'd stay away, not smirk all over me and find out how I make a living before they decide if I'm good enough to be bored to death by their twaddle. I don't need their bloody approval - nor yours!"

"So why didn't you tell us all that you're a busker?"

Ralph switched the case to his other hand and looked down the street at the hurrying crowds to find a reason.

She had him there.

"Yes, well I suppose I'm just as full of shit as anyone else come to think of it. Thank you for pointing that out."

She almost smiled.

"So would you allow a self-confessed toadie buy you a pizza - with his hard-won pennies as a highly trained, dazzlingly-talented and slightly damp busker - or beggar if you prefer?"

Her outfit pulled eyes their way in the little bright red and green, smoky pizzeria.

"I think you've outshone me tonight," admitted Ralph, aware of his denim and worn trainers. "But what these people don't know yet is that the 'battered' look is all the rage up-town."

"This is up-town."

"Wrong town. I was thinking of Luton - the new spangle of the Fashion World. They're breaking away from boring old style and branching out into unexplored territory."

"Denim?"

"Only to the untrained eye. Thank you. They do good ice-creams here. They look brilliant but I've never had one."

"You didn't like my friends at the party then?"

"I only had a superficial impression remember, I spent most of the time talking to you I'm happy to say. But didn't like that git-in-the-suit. Does he always talk to people like they're a plateful of leftovers? Or is he just amazingly constipated?"

"Shh! That was Tom! He's not like that really."

"So how did you know it was him I was talking about?"

"He was just..."

"Ill? Sick? Dropped on his head as a kid? What?"

She laughed, then went serious again.

"No he was just, well, jealous I suppose... suppose I was going out with him... and he gets very protective."

"And who protects you from him... when he's being protective?"

"He thought I was with you."

So did I.

"I'd like a House Special - whatever that is. How long have you been busking?"

"Since I got my first rattle. Do you fancy pepperoni?"

They ordered. They swapped resumes and brief CVs until the food arrived.

"Tom's an architect. It's what he always wanted to be."

"Oh, him again - so how long since you and him stopped 'supposedly' going out for him to be still patrolling around, beating his chest?"

Uh oh, clumsy git.

She was staring at the table and looked suddenly close to tears. The food had arrived and she stared at it as if decoding the mushrooms. There had to be a way of shifting the current quickly without sounding callous... No, too late... her hand went up to her forehead. Oh Christ. Ralph didn't know what he should do but he deserted his 'Margherita' (with extra cheese), went round to her side and put an arm over her stooped shoulders to reassure her that the world wasn't as bad as he knew it to be - but this broke the dam and the tears came.

Between sobs he heard that someone called 'she' - and a few other words he never used himself - had arrived at 'their' party and that 'they' had been upstairs (doing what, Ralph was dying to know but didn't feel it appropriate to ask). 'It' had apparently been going on 'for ages' and she'd known 'all along'.

She had 'caught Tom out' before but 'this was it' and she 'never wanted to see him again' although she did 'love him', 'if only he wouldn't lie to her, but then everyone lies, even you' and 'I want him back'.

The pizzas had congealed. Ralph was totally confused as to what to say or do for the best. He didn't let go of her with his right arm but he tore off a section of 'Margherita' with his left and started eating it and thinking about Tom and hating him some more.

"He phoned up this morning. I told him who you were - or who I thought you were - and told him I was going to the theatre with you. He thinks you're a real musician. He's an architect. He's only 24 and he's doing really well..." Ralph really needed to hear this... "and he knows he's going to get on. We work for the same firm..." she sniffed and wiped at her eyes. "What about you? Haven't you ever tried to... well, have you ever tried?"

That was a bit below the belt.

"Getting out of bed is an effort for me so you could say I've fought long and hard to get where I am today. Up and dressed."

"Have you got no ambition?"

"One or two. But nothing I could earn a living by. Nothing they would pay me to do. I'm a qualified draughtsman - or person - if that's any good, and I've had a year at a music college where I did some interesting stuff and met some interesting folk, but here I am. All ready for life's merry roulette to gamble away a few more of my years. What about you? How did you get into 'interiors'? If that's the right way to put it. What pulled you that way?"

"Can't remember - but that's how I met Tom…"

"Him again! All conversations lead to Tom! Let's talk about something else. You'll have to stand up to him you know - don't let him mess you about like that - play him at his own game for a while maybe, if you want, or get rid of him if he makes you unhappy. Life's too short to spend it chasing around after some mirage. Especially if the competition's steep."

The light-brown eyes were full of anger, "She is no competition!"

"She? I meant him! Such love as that cannot be replaced, I've seen it before - self-infatuation, and no one else counts. He probably couldn't love anyone else if…"

"Well that's where you're wrong! And what do you know about it? You don't think I'm going to finish with him for somebody like you do you?"

"There isn't anybody like me - I've looked. Finish with him for yourself, I mean, he obviously makes you unhappy, you don't need him leading you around…"

She stood up. The tears had gone - burned away.

"You'd best get back to your fiddle and your... busking, thanks for your gracious company. When I need advice from you, I'll let you know."

She left, returned for her bag, and left again.

The people across the way also seemed to prefer their pizzas congealed and were waiting to see what

Ralph would do. He watched them to see what they would do. They ate their cold pizzas in silence.

Ralph ordered one of the huge ice-creams advertised on the back of the menu.

It tasted like its cardboard image might have done, but he ate it anyway.

*

As the rain fell in the night, some of the smaller producers went bankrupt as they could no longer get returns on investments quick enough and shut up shop. The larger ones bought them up, taking over premises and machinery and, sometimes, the people needed to run it. DCL did quite well gobbling up a few minor competitors, but even DCL had to close down some production centres, lay off some folk. They didn't want to but the markets seemed to demand it if they were going to keep the returns up. Some minor projects might still run if the investment had already happened rather than lose it all. Some producers had to go so far as to destroy the products rather than let prices fall so far - food, consumer goods, tools - all had to go. Shame really.

Chapter 14

After a couple of days, Ralph had called round to return a brooch, apologise and talk some more. It wasn't her brooch: he wasn't really surprised at this as he'd found it on a train somewhere about a month ago, but he had thought he had better check just in case.

Apparently, Tom had moved back in. He was out but Angie didn't want to go for a drink and generally didn't overwhelm Ralph with welcome.

But then, a week or so later, she had come around.

She had finished with Tom again, but 'for good this time' and Ralph had taken her out on the town - having threatened Allan with his own cooking for a month if he didn't lend out some of his gear and some cash until the following week.

And a pattern was set: Ralph was there when needed - but not otherwise. Tom would return contrite and would always be taken back. Angela didn't tell any of her friends about Ralph nor did she ever take him to the places where she might meet any of them. Ralph was aware of this and knew the reason but there wasn't much he could do about it: he wasn't going anywhere and she didn't want to get there with him. That was all.

A while later, Allan had been late back to the house one evening when Anna had called round. She and Ralph were drinking cans of beer and watching the soaps until Allan got back.

The doorbell went and Ralph knew who it would be. Angela was standing on the doorstep. She looked cold.

"Alright if I come in?"

She always said that as if half-expecting the world to slam its door in her face. As if he ever could say 'no'.

Anna hadn't met her before and turned to greet her, curious to meet the mysterious woman Allan had told her about - and the reason Ralph had taken to staying in most nights and moping about the place the rest of the time like a sick dog.

She was surprised to see Angela's unhappy face.

"Hello!" Anna said brightly.

"Hello, are you Allan's girlfriend?"

Anna was taken aback. She wouldn't normally describe herself as someone else's anything but... if labels were required... "Yes that's right. Nice to meet you."

The enthusiasm was apparently not reciprocal and the proffered can of lager was refused.

Ralph came back from fetching a bottle of wine - Anna wondered whereabouts in the kitchen he had been hiding it - and poured out some glasses.

"What's happened?" she heard Ralph ask quietly - he knew she would not have come around if there had not been some catastrophe. Angie replied in a low mumble interspersed with sniffs. Anna was still staring at the television screen but her every ounce of being was concentrated into trying to hear. All she heard was about Tom's latest escapade and an episode of Angela's difficulties at work and she sneaked a look to see how Ralph was taking this.

The look on his face convinced her it was worse than she had thought. And that Allan had been wrong. Not that this staggered her. She realised she had met Angela of various types before and this was just another of the species.

Ralph, from what she knew of Ralph, and judging by her own experiences, would need help.

But then Allan had arrived and Anna and he had gone straight out.

Allan was dismissive. He usually was of other people's worries, she had noticed.

"Oh he just lets her drone on to him until its bed time. Poor sod - it's the only way he can score. I only hope she's worth it."

"What's she drone on about?"

"Oh anything - her job, men, money, the weather, you name it, all gets full coverage..."

"Does he like that kind of thing then?"

"What, sex? I think so."

"No, talking to someone like that?"

"Don't know if he actually likes it. He told me - he uses it all the time, has women queuing up I tell you. Bit of soft soap and he's away. Wish I could do it. Glad I don't have to."

"Is he really like that?"

"Yes! Why, what did you think? It's alright. She gets to have a good moan, and he gets his leg-over. What's the problem?"

"I don't think that's true."

"You don't have to believe me. But I know Ralph better than you do."

"I think she's a leech."

"A what?"

"A leech. Pond-life. Suck you dry."

"I'm sure Ralph doesn't mind that."

"That isn't what I meant. He's a soft touch. You ought to warn him."

"What? That he might get laid? I'd do better warning Angie. I don't think it would be too much of a shock for him - it has happened before, amazingly enough. He's not exactly sweet and innocent. And he knows when he's onto a good thing."

"He's been bloody miserable lately."

"He was born bloody miserable. He's happy that way."

"How come you and him are mates?"

Allan shrugged. "Don't know. He likes me I think. Looks up to me."

Anna looked at him closely. But he was being

absolutely serious.

The following morning Anna decided to interfere in what was not her business - her own business being more than usually uninteresting. Allan had gone for the bus and she was rummaging, carefully, in the fridge, when Ralph blundered, bleary-eyed, into the kitchen.

"Hi Anna." He started manufacturing a cup of coffee from the remnants of various packages.

"Oh Hello. How's romance treating you?"

"Fine. Have you seen the kettle?"

The kettle was in the sink. He lifted it out, filled it and lit the gas.

She tried again. "So, how's the love life?"

"Fine - why?"

"She still here or has she gone back to Tom?"

Ralph stopped what he was doing, the teaspoonful of coffee poised.

"What's up with you this morning?" he said warily.

"Just interested. Have you solved all her problems yet or has she thought up a few more to keep you going?"

"What do you know about it?"

"Enough. I've been wondering what's been wrong with you lately."

"And what has been?"

"You've been like a bear with a sore head actually, putting it politely."

"That's my business isn't it? Go away, Anna, you're annoying me - why are you annoying me? You've been spending too much time with Allan, that's your trouble."

"Well we can't spend any time with you these days - you mope about the place like a herring."

"A herring?"

"Best I could think of. Stop changing the subject. Look at yourself. You've got to cheer up."

"Which is it then? Do I look at myself or do I cheer up?"

"Somebody was doing that to me once - just dumping all their problems onto me - I was as miserable as hell for ages until I figured out why."

"She isn't 'just dumping all her problems onto me', as you put it, we happen to get on rather well. You just don't understand because we spend time actually talking to each other. You probably find that quite weird, you and Allan. Have you two ever had a conversation or are you still working round to it?"

"We're working round to it. Sorry if you disapprove…"

"That's not what I was saying… yes, Angie's got a lot of worries, she's very sensitive…"

"So's a rat-trap…"

"Not everyone's as sorted-out as you are, Anna, some people do get into a mess…"

"So you get in it with them?"

"You're too bloody hard-faced to understand."

"I'm too bloody old not to. How many times have I had some leech crawling on me and called it 'a relationship'? Or a friendship! People can use you, you know and you don't see it 'til afterwards..."

"Anna," Ralph closed the fridge door, having found some milk that was still liquid, "tell Allan. Don't tell me. Coming from you two this is all a bit rich. And if you want to talk 'relationships', I'd rather ones that mean some pain than ones that meant nothing at all."

Anna was a bit stumped for a reply.

Ralph went back upstairs.

Relations between them had been slightly frosty since then. Allan noticed this and asked the reason but by unspoken consensus they had only said something vague about 'a row'. His curiosity was satisfied with this.

Anna had moved into quite a comfortable house, a squat, occupied by some others and there was space so she had invited Allan to move in.

Allan had invited Ralph. Ralph had considered leaving the overpriced, cold and grubby house to share the free, much warmer squat - with Allan - and stayed where he was.

He had seen Allan and Anna together a few times after that - like at the college 'do' where Allan had met that posh idiot, Caroline, at the end of term. Ralph had had to leave the term before but Allan had bought him a ticket.

Later, he had heard that Allan was with Caroline - a match made in heaven if ever there was one, he had thought then that the squat was empty and that Anna had moved away. He had decided to move when he could get no more work and the bills were fighting their way in through the letter-box.

He had phoned Angie to tell her.

He knew immediately that Tom was there by the tone of her voice: cold.

"Tonight?" she said, to his question. "Well, yes, actually, there's a dinner-dance on with the Firm. With Tom."

She smiled over at Tom, who smiled back. He liked it when others tried to ask Angela out. He knew loads of them fancied her. He also liked the way she put him before any of her women friends as well.

"Oh well, I just phoned to say I'm doing a moonlight, that's all. I'm going to that squat I was telling you about, remember? Wild Rose Court."

Angie was looking at the dress she had just bought, hanging on the back of the chair. It looked wonderful on her. She liked fine things and knew Tom appreciated them too. Why had she got enmeshed with someone like Ralph with his unpaid bills and moonlighting?

"Yes, I remember. You should be alright there."

"Can I see you before I go?"

"Well I am busy, right now. And it's not far."

"No. Alright, I can tell I'm in the doghouse. But I've got to go, I'm broke."

"That's nothing new."

"Well thanks for the moral support." She could

joke lightly about it, of course, because she didn't know what it was like. How could he expect her to know?

"Goodbye then."

"Goodbye."

He should have known better than to have phoned, or to say anything when Tom was there. She was never her usual self when he was around.

He packed his bag and left the house.

He had not seen or heard from her for weeks since then and had tried not to think about her in all that time. The squat had been empty until Anna's unexpected and rather dramatic return, but he had not done anything to bring in more people. He hadn't wanted to be around people. Another bar job, off the cards, another couple of flings with people whose names he couldn't recall and who probably wouldn't remember his - and now here she was, out of the blue. Looking so out of place in the squat.

But during those weeks, from the kindness of distance, the dots, patches and blurs had started to merge. They had blended, shaped and fused into patterns until the picture they formed was bitter and clear.

He recovered from the shock of seeing her.

"And what are you doing here?" he asked.

His tone took her by surprise and put her on her guard.

"Come on in then," he put the empty bucket down and used the last of the water in the bottles by the sink to wash the glue off his hands. Anna and Reny seemed to have gone.

"I've come to see you," this was querulous and she sniffed to reinforce the message.

"Oh yeah?" he dried his hands. "Why's that?"

There was silence for a brief space.

"Ralph, I've come to see you!"

"So, what's wrong then?"

"What do you mean?"

"Well there's got to be something wrong hasn't there or you don't know who I am. What is it this time?"

"Well you haven't been round to see me either."

"After that phone call? Wouldn't dare! It was pretty obvious you didn't want to see me - so what are you doing here? Has that prize dickhead you're in love with left you again? Or is your glittering career boring you again? Or maybe... just for variety, maybe that set of vultures you laughingly know as friends are getting their hooks in you again or..."

Angie had got up and was halfway to the door.

"Oh don't go... I'm hoping to get the film-rights... and I haven't got a telly to watch any other drama..."

She turned to glare at him - did fury or tears do that to her eyes?

"Even a total mug like me gets tired you know... you coming around for a dose of ego-drops from me. But you don't have any problems you don't love and where the hell are you when I need you? Is this what you're like with other people, or is it just me who gets the down-trodden waif performance... Shit!"

He ducked just in time as the glass she had snatched up from the table smashed on the wall behind him. "You bastard!"

"Oh that was your good side? On bad days, you throw glasses at people? Well you keep all of it."

He turned away, expecting her to leave. But she wasn't going yet.

"Sorry! I got you wrong. It must have been really boring listening to me before you could get what you want. If you had let me know, I'd have shut up sooner. I thought you were better than that but I might have known you're all the bloody same. Tom might be a bastard but at least he doesn't pretend otherwise!"

She had turned on the last words and marched down the stairwell.

Stung to the quick, Ralph went after her. "For Christ's sake Angie, it was hardly like that was it? You never came around unless you needed a shoulder to cry on!"

"And which bit of me were you needing?"

"All of you, if you must know," he'd said before he could help it. "But we... I... we slept together because we wanted to, didn't we... I thought... We both did..."

"And I thought we both talked about my worries because we wanted to. You never said otherwise – 'til now. You never walked out."

"No, but you always did."

Angie looked round at the squalor around her and shivered. Ralph followed her gaze and said nothing. He could hardly blame her. Love me, love my hovel?

"Is there somebody else now? Allan said you were living with someone?"

"No there isn't." His voice was harsh. "Come on, we can talk upstairs. I'm a miserable sod sometimes and you took me by surprise."

She put her arms round him and he kissed her, hugging her close, still halfway down the stairs, until they had to separate to regain their balance, which let them laugh. They went back upstairs

*

The next morning, Angela woke and tried to guess if Ralph was awake. His breathing was slow and regular. Their breath made thin smoke in the morning, Angela leaned over and switched the electric fire on again and rearranged the blankets to get warm. Then she got up quietly and went to the bathroom. Her mascara was smudged into panda's eyes. She got out her cotton-wool and make-up remover, wiped her face clean, re-did her eyes and dabbed a little perfume here and there. The bathroom was cold and Spartan and there was no water in the taps.

The ugliness of the squalor was more painful by day; the rough patchwork of old rugs and bits of carpet on the floorboards, and the ill-matched bits of furniture rescued from skips.

She closed her mind to this as she went back to Ralph's room where the 'curtain' was still across the window and the shadows hid the worst. He was sprawled across the mattress, the bedding around his middle, his shoulders bare. She got back into bed next to him and lay there, wondering if Tom had been round last night and found her gone.

Ralph woke her again with a kiss on the back of her neck. He knew she liked that. He massaged her neck and shoulders and moved slowly down her back, his hands and tongue like an electric shock on her skin. She pretended to be still asleep and he carried on, waking her up all over.

They lay in the shadows later, close and warm, feeling pretty good. Ralph had decided that he wouldn't go into work that day. She kissed his forehead and he smiled, eyes still closed. "You got any work yet?"

His smile disappeared. "Not just yet." The bar-job or the night watch shifts wouldn't count, he knew that.

"I just wondered."

"Pulling pints is my only vocation. My birth right."

"What about your music? You could teach?"

"I tried that. They closed the place down. Hate kids anyway."

"It's a pity to waste your talent."

"Not me who's wasting it. There's just no demand for it these days. If Mozart came back they'd stick him on a training scheme digging holes. Or off with his head. Or off with his benefit in this enlightened day and age. In fact, he probably has. And they have."

"Don't be silly. Genius always emerges."

"It certainly does. And spends its time working out

how to make three Oxo cubes and half a loaf last until the end of the week."

"What about private lessons?"

"Nobody can afford them."

"Rich people can."

"They already know how to fiddle. They wouldn't let me in the door never mind near their precious offspring. They'd think I was after the silver. And I would be an' all." He always found himself reverting to caricature when he was with Angela.

"You're being very negative. If you really want to do something you always can."

Ralph opened his eyes and went hunting through the blankets, "Was that Tom? It sounded like him? Didn't know he was here! Sounded like one of his platitudes - A Platitude A Day Keeps Reality Away?"

"But it's true! People make it, don't they?"

"Some. Hardly any. Most with private incomes or with rich sponsors calling the tune. Mostly men."

"Well, most women can't do those sorts of things..."

"Well you can see why, can't you... imagine it - hold the baby for a minute would you, Ludwig, he's dribbling on me symphony, or a note propped up on ye oldie kitcheney tabley – 'Dear William, there's a pig's head in the fridge, I'm off down the library to finish me sonnets, yours ever, Mrs Shakespeare.'"

"I thought you said he was gay?"

"Only sometimes. I was just making the point. It's a bit tricky if you haven't got time and money. Money mainly because that buys you time."

"You forgot talent."

"Everyone's got that. Until drudgery grinds it out. We're not going to quarrel, are we?"

"No. What about that drawing stuff you were doing?"

He smiled. "The draughtsmanship scam? That was a real wheeze - get myself qualified just when they don't want anyone to draw anymore. They want computer drawings. Great timing. They all decided they could make more money out of nerve-gas and you can't draw nerve gas. Least I can't. Want some tea?" He got out of bed and pulled some clothes on.

It annoyed him when she was like this. All his defences put under pressure. It was hard enough just to keep going never mind bring about major changes in life. He went through to the kitchen, hoping they wouldn't end up just bickering all day.

When he'd gone, she stretched out under the cool sheet, every muscle tingling. God, she felt good - pity he had to go and spoil it. Then she saw the dark, round-edged patch of damp high up on the wall. She closed her eyes. She wanted a cup of coffee really, like at home, but she knew he wouldn't have any.

She remembered what Tom had told her about Wild Rose Court and the plans that were down for it. She wondered if she should tell Ralph. That would probably annoy him again because it meant talking about Tom. There was nothing they could do about it anyway. And it wasn't their house after all. And it was

Tom's big chance. Ralph wouldn't understand that. He didn't have any ambition.

"We're going to have to move soon," he said. She had got up and wandered into the kitchen, wrapped in one of his shirts.

"What do you mean? They knew already?"

"Notices came through weeks ago. And they've been down, sniffing around with tripods and clipboards. Dunno what they're going to do with it. Turn it into a car-park I should think, or a hole in the ground so they can sell off the dirt. Souvenirs. Or maybe a nice cosy missile base."

"Don't be miserable."

"Oh sorry, am I being miserable? S'pose it's only my home they're taking from me. Suppose one should always look on the bright side? Chin-up and all that? Well, at least it'll be a relief to get away from the rats. There, how's that? Aren't I a little ray of sunshine? And it can be quite nice living in the gutter because sometimes it doesn't rain. How am I doing?"

"Can they just chuck you out - just like that?" That wasn't what Tom had been saying.

"As far as I know."

"You could refuse to go?"

"Well yes - and get dragged out by the scuffers and done over. Great. We've all been there."

What was it Tom had said?

"They'd lose money if they had to wait for you to go."

It was very tight anyway, Tom had said, the money

they stood to make was only just enough to make it worthwhile, one more hitch to the project and the approval would be withdrawn and Tom's big chance will have gone. But Ralph didn't seem to know that.

"Yes, but peanuts to them," he replied. "They'd have to keep the builders and whatever waiting a few days maybe but what's that to them? It's a massive, great company apparently. You couldn't stop that without muscle. And we haven't got any."

Angie could have explained the situation more fully - that the massive great company was on the edge of the financial equivalent of a massive great coronary - too much gone out, not enough coming in, and a great and dangerous gap threatening to open up and suck it down - but decided not to. Tom would be so pleased to hear that there wasn't going to be any big problem after all so they could go ahead and book the date and sign up contractors and all that... and he could stop behaving like a scalded bear. The people here seemed quite happy to move on - there was only Ralph here anyway at the moment and he was used to the rough life.

"Do you like concerts?" he said, coming over to her and folding his arms around her so she nearly spilled her tea. "Because there's one coming to the Park on the 21st in support of you-know-what, which I know you don't agree with but it would be good anyway. Especially if the sun comes out. We're all going - the lot over the road you haven't met. Fancy it?"

"Sounds nice - but I'm not sure what I'm doing."

He released her from his arms as he remembered her other life.

"Yeah, right, but we're all going for the day - a mob outing - and you're invited if you like, that's all."

"When is it?" she was suddenly interested. All of them away? Her mind was a set trap for the answer.

"The 21st... half-price if…"

"Great! That'd be great, I'll come. If I can. I'll meet you there, it'll be really good."

Her enthusiasm took him by surprise.

"I've got to be going now Ralph…Thanks for... it was nice seeing you again…"

"Nice, the woman says! I could have sworn it was bloody fantastic... do you have to go?" He unbuttoned the shirt, slowly, and followed his hand down the row of buttons with his mouth.

When she eventually left, she turned at the gateway and blew him a kiss. He laughed, caught and held it, and watched her walk away.

Chapter 15

When Anna awoke, she was alone in Reny's basement room. There was a message on the empty milk carton, 'Dear Anna,' it said - rather unnecessarily it seemed in the circumstances - 'Gone to work, See you later'. He'd signed it 'Reny', which again seemed a bit superfluous.

She was starving. And lonely. And cold.

She got back to find Ralph alone and leaning on the sink halfway through a doorstep of the last of the loaf she'd bought. The margarine tub was open and the smeared knife lay in the crumbs on the table.

Men!

He stopped chewing and looked at the open, empty wrapper the loaf had been in - willing another loaf, or another anything edible that he had bought to materialise there. One didn't.

"Oh thanks Ralph, that was my bloody breakfast."

"I'm sorry - I was hungry."

"Oh that's alright then - I was only going to eat it 'cos I like the sound of chewing."

"I thought you'd gone to work?"

"So you helped yourself? Great."

"It's stale anyway."

"Oh, I am sorry, if I'd known you were going to nick it I'd have bought a fresh one. You just struggle through my horrible stale breakfast and I'll sit and watch your agony."

"You just missed Angie."

"Oh no! It's one big disappointment after another and it's only ten o'clock. How will I get through the day? And look at the mess you've made."

"It was no show-house when I got here. And about Angie - you were wrong, y'know."

"There's a first for everything... I want my breakfast."

"So did I. Sorry. I was hungry and the bread was just there... don't hit me, I'll be back before you know it," he dug a coin out of a pocket and brandished it aloft, "with delicacies undreamed of, in a rich wine sauce, on golden platters, with cakes of spice..."

"And could you get some margarine while you're at it..." He was gone.

He was alright really. In small doses. For a bloke.

Anna went into the 'lounge'. The walls were blank except for a few posters and a patch of mould which kept growing back however many times they cleaned it. It looked a bit like a bush growing in the corner there. Or more like the shadow or silhouette of one. Pity they couldn't train damp patches to spread to a pretty pattern or picture. That was an idea.

There were some old tins of paint still under the sink and she fetched them out: sticky tins and two brushes - one still usable, the other like a rock. She prised off the lids with the crumby knife. Black, blue and white, but not enough of either to do the wall. She poured them all together into the white tin and mixed them to a marble and then to a deep turquoise-y shade.

She split up some old papers and spread them close to the wall – not necessary really but if it was worth doing...

She stood back and looked at the wall. Bushes? Trees? Roots below and branches overhead. Foliage and a smoky trunk down the left hand-side - not straight but curved and knotted the way real trees grow. She dipped the brush and swept the paint on in a thin, shallow, almost vertical curve, then another, broader and bolder and another, building up the trunk of the tree. Straighter or curvier, the lower part coiling into roots along the base of the wall, thicker here and there for shadows in the bark. She ran to get a damp cloth and dabbed off dribbles as the paint ran to collect in the lowest edges and threatened to run.

It was drying to a lighter shade, the damp patch blending in. She got one of the boxes to stand on to do the leaves and branches.

"Hope we're not disturbing you," the loud voice behind her nearly made her fall as the man walked cheerfully into the room with a clipboard, looking round the walls and ceiling. "Hope you're not too busy but some of us have work to do."

"What are you doing? Who are you?" taken by

surprise she could only try to hide her fear. She got down off the box and got ready for trouble.

He ignored her, marked something on his clipboard with his pen and indicated to the second man who had followed him in to go through to what was Ralph's room. He mused around the kitchen looking at the remnants of 'fittings'.

"You lot shouldn't be here you know, you've had plenty of warning to get out. How many of you are there?" he asked. She didn't answer. "Not that it matters. We'll just do our job if you don't mind."

"I do mind. I live here."

He snorted. "Well in that case, we'll do our job if you do mind. We've tolerated you..." and he hesitated over the word, "...people... for long enough."

Ralph came in with a carrier bag. He saw Tom standing in the kitchen, measuring and writing and stopped. Tom didn't look up immediately.

Anna said, "This jerk and his mate are here to measure the place up. An official housebreaker."

Tom turned from checking the skirting board for any bad signs of cracks or subsidence. He and Ralph knew each other instantly.

"Ah, hello, it's the maestro isn't it? Strange we should meet here..."

He glanced around the down-trodden room and his eyes came to rest on Anna and he looked her up and down.

"Are you slumming it or just experimenting with the delights of Low-Life?"

178

They both reached him at the same time and the clipboard went flying. Jim, who'd gone through to measure the other room, rushed back in to see what was happening but didn't seem keen to rush to Tom's rescue or to wreak revenge on his attackers. Quite the reverse. His hand went over his mouth as he pretended to scratch his chin.

Tom straightened up warily when they'd stood back.

"If you want any more there's plenty where it came from," he was told.

"I could report you for that."

"Go ahead, you'll have the law behind you - vermin always have. Better crawl out of here and go running to them."

Tom was still breathing heavily. They had both slapped him a lot harder than they looked as if they could but he didn't want to lose face and they wouldn't dare do anything too extreme. He got out the measuring tape and, only wishing there was some other way of reaching the floor, knelt to one skirting board and signalled to Jim to take the other end into the kitchen.

Walking to the kitchen, with his back to Tom, Jim released the delighted grin he had been keeping under control since seeing Tom reel under attack from the two under-fed down-and-outs. Ralph saw, and guessed the reason. He would hate to have to work under a nasty, pretentious fart like Tom.

They finished measuring the living room and went to check out the bathroom.

"I hope you weren't defending my honour, Ralph."

"Sod yours, I was defending mine."

"Cheek! Didn't know you had any. How do you know him?"

"Long story. Not interesting."

"What shall we do now?"

"Cry?"

"A real action-man aren't you?"

Tom came back in.

"There's dust on your knees," Anna pointed out, helpfully.

He ignored her and refrained from dusting it off. They followed them upstairs and Tom, leading the way, put his entire foot through the rotten stair they had all learned to avoid.

"Do you enjoy your work?" was the polite enquiry as he limped the rest of the way, trying to hide the fact that he'd skinned his ankle.

Ralph and Anna followed them around as they measured and investigated and noted down.

"Hope you don't mind us watching but you can't be too careful these days," said Ralph, moving an entirely worthless lamp out of harm's way. "How much do they pay you for doing this? Enough I hope?"

He got no answer. Jim would have liked to have told him but knew it wouldn't go down well to be seen fraternising with the enemy so he kept quiet. The enemy trailed after them, doing their best to be annoying. All pretty petty perhaps but what else was there to do? Anna went over to tell the other household what was happening and they came over.

By the time the two intruders left, they had collected an attentive audience who had followed them with critical acclaim around each of the two houses until Tom wanted to kill someone. Jim recognised that he would be the most likely target for Tom to choose on whom to vent his anger so he enjoyed Tom's annoyance to the full, while it lasted, trying to keep a straight face.

He'd tell the others at work about this - they'd love it. The bit about him getting roughed up was the best.

In the first house, Tom glared at the makeshift electrics and made a note. Then he turned a tap on. There was no response whatsoever. The little group stood and watched to see what he would do. He looked inside the cupboard under the sink. "You've got mice!" he blurted in disgust, confronted too near the nose with the evidence. Exclamations of disbelief and enlightenment greeted his proclamation, 'I thought we'd eaten them all,' and 'Tut tut, shocking,' and 'I always wondered where the mouse-shit came from,' and so on while Jim contemplated his fingernails and Tom went from one level of anger to another.

He found the pipe he was looking for under the sink and idly tapped it with his pen wondering why it wasn't working. "Nice bit of workmanship that - you can always tell a professional."

"'S'what my granddad always said - if it don't

work, bash t'bugger with pen - always does the trick that..."

Tom put the pen away and walked off purposefully into the next room. It was a cupboard so he went on into the toilet room.

The taps in all the sinks were dry. There was a bouquet of buckets and other containers in the hallway. Some still full of water, others empty.

"Where do you get water?" he asked, without thinking.

"We use instant granules."

"We grow it."

"Gets delivered wit' milk"

"Is that water? We've been conned! The dealer swore it was Gin."

Tom made another note, signalled for Jim to follow and went over to the other house. Some followed, others stayed to discuss the situation.

The heckling spirit had left them and they sat around contemplating yet another enforced move and the uninviting alternatives left open to them. There was the return to their Bed & Breakfast 'homes' with the attendant loneliness and drifting this required; a return to unwelcoming, sometimes dangerous, always stifling but often non-existent parental homes. There was the long trek around the city to find another house to open up and stay in while they were allowed if, and this was getting increasingly unlikely, they could find one that wasn't already packed to the rafters, there was the search for scarce, squalid, over-priced and lonely bed-sitters - where an income was needed before you could have an address - and vice versa. There was the street or the embankment - where at least they would have lots of company.

There was resistance.

"We should have beaten those bastards up and thrown them out while we had the chance," was Reny's opinion on his return home.

"There'd be ten more here tomorrow – plus filth!"

"We mustn't use violence."

"So what would you do? Sing to them?"

"If they sent police-women to chuck us out, would you be happy?"

"We could occupy and have a sit-in?"

"Oh Christ - let's all have a love-in while we're at it..."

"That'd be better than getting done for assault..."

"And when they attack, what do we do, strangle them with your love-beads?"

"Scrapping amongst ourselves won't get us very far."

"No, but it's fun."

"If there were more of us... they couldn't drag us all away."

"Well there isn't more of us, is there? We haven't got public sympathy either."

"Send 'em a picture of Reny's acne - that'd have them in tears."

"Ha fuckin' ha."

"We could tell the papers what's going on."

"They know. They couldn't give a shit."

"Can't think why - loads of people who own newspapers are homeless."

"It was only a suggestion."

"They'd probably run a competition - kill a squatter, win a metro..."

"Alright, alright, you come up with something then. It just might be worth organising something."

They saw Tom and Jim come out of the house opposite, get in the car and drive away. The others came over and they agreed to meet later to make a decision, when they had had more time to think about it, about what they would do - or if it was worth doing anything at all?

Ralph looked around for Anna but she had gone into the other room and closed the door.

She felt tight around the throat. Being tired and hungry didn't help but the thought of another move... alone again and homeless... there was a kind of pressure on her lungs and she took a deep breath to relieve it but that only allowed the weak tears to come... Those complacent bastards with their measuring tapes and smug smiles! There was nothing they could do - just onto the next hovel and the one after that and no money and the worst work and time racing at a gallop - towards what? She closed her eyes and forced back the tears. There was a knock at the door - she didn't answer it.

"Anna? Have you ever had a toasted treacle sandwich?" There was silence. What was that idiot on about now? "...With cheese?"

"Go away Ralph, I'm not in the mood."

She thought he'd gone but then he said, "Do you think I am?"

She hesitated.

"Come in then." There was no answer. She opened the door but he'd gone. In the kitchen, Ralph had left his early morning shopping and a cold treacle sandwich with some cheese crumbled onto it. It tasted wonderful.

*

Tom wasn't in a good mood. Jim could tell by the way he crashed his gears and took corners on the edge of his wheels.

"Bunch of bloody, bug-ridden nowts. God, wouldn't I love to pour a load of kerosene over their rat-pit, plug up the holes and put a match to the whole show. Bloody dropouts. I'm so looking forward to seeing them turfed out."

Jim said nothing. He knew he was supposed to laugh or snort in agreement or similar, as usual, when Tom was holding forth about something, but this time he didn't feel like going along with him as he usually did. Tom glanced at him but he was driving too quickly to be able to figure out Jim's expression.

"Well? You sympathise with that lot, do you?"

"They've got to live somewhere I suppose?"

"Oh, don't give me that! You saw the state of the place. Give them a palace, it'd be a slum in a week. They ruin good houses they do. Sitting around in their own dirt. They've no right to be there."

"There are quite a few homeless people about though, aren't there?"

"Look, don't believe everything you read in the papers. They choose to live like that? Fine, let them. They could all go home couldn't they?"

Jim considered whether to leave it at that but then said, "I had a bit of bother once - had to stay in a hostel. When I was getting divorced. Hostel they called it. Doss house more like. Crowded. Dirty..." He watched the buildings flying past the car window, remembering.

"Well there you are! Proves my point!" Tom jumped on the evidence. "Look at you now. Proves it. You got yourself out and fixed up and everything. You made it! Show's it can be done. Sheer drive and guts is all you need and if people haven't got that... then they deserve what they get!"

Jim kept his mouth closed and kept looking out of the window. He wondered how hard and from how far Tom had had to push.

Sitting on the polythene Tom had asked him, very politely, to put between his dusty work clothes and the upholstery of Tom's new car, Jim didn't feel as if he had 'made it'. Drive and guts didn't pay bills. His own daughter had plenty of both but if it wasn't for the grant system she would never have got into college. Jim didn't even earn enough to support her there.

He remembered some of the faces he had known when at the hostel. The advice they had given him on how to survive. The ones who would never work again - their old skills not wanted, their willingness to learn new ones ignored. Their chances growing ever slimmer, as time passed, of ever being able to get back on the treadmill, which was the highest hope their life offered. Or had ever offered.

"Not everyone's so lucky," he said.

"Course not - survival of the fittest and all that. Natural," Tom had never actually read any Darwin but he misquoted him out of context with confidence. "Too many people and not enough of anything else. Breed like rabbits, too, what do they expect?"

"The royals breed but they don't go short," muttered Jim, but now they were back at DCL and Tom was concentrating on sweeping stylishly into the car park. He pulled into a space, jerked to a halt and got out.

The space didn't have his name on it but he looked forward to the day when it would.

"Right, you bring along those sheets and we'll lay it on the line to the old boy right away, don't give him any of the 'worker's united' stuff though, it might not go down very well..." Tom marched on ahead.

Jim slowed down and took his time. He was biting his tongue and counting up to ten which did nothing at all for his looks. He had a handy left-hook and knew it, but there was the pay-check - such as it was - at the end of the week, which he needed. He kept counting.

By the time he got to the lifts, Tom was being matey again and started telling the one about the virgin and the rugby team so Jim was able to yawn, very realistically, half-way through the punch-line which put Tom in the sulks again.

"Ah there you are," Arthur was feeling bored and lonely. Almost lonely enough to be pleased to see Tom. The new secretary had not turned out at all as he had expected: all efficiency and work and not as chatty or as comfortable as Mrs T had been, nor as consistent with the cups of tea and the sympathetic listening he was used to and missed. Not enough women's intuition to see to his needs, he had decided, and she was so serious! Especially over this latest little project - she seemed to have got a bee in her bonnet over that for some reason. Women!

Various executive toys Clara had given him for various birthdays and Christmases littered his desk. They had clicked and puzzled him to new levels of ennui over the years.

"Come in, come in!" He was glad of someone to talk to. Oh no, it was Tom. God, that suit!

Tom presented Arthur with the lists of figures and estimates and started to explain. Arthur waved him away. He had been dealing in marketing buildings since before Tom had had his own play-pen to re-possess.

"So No. 3 is out then?" Arthur concluded from a quick glance at the figures involved.

He remembered the summer house and its patterned glass colouring the sunlight. Then forgot it.

Business was business after all. One had to prioritise.

"Yes," agreed Tom, seizing on the chance to elaborate in front of Jim. "There would be a total of four executive apartments in the other house, as you can see, which was the maximum decided upon that we could sell at this price in a short enough period in today's climate, and No. 5 is in a considerably better state structure wise."

He was waving his pen instructively back and forth across the diagrams, leaning over Arthur's shoulder.

Irritated, Arthur closed the file. "So we just need to run up the site plans and that's it. But we'll have to get the place vacant soon. Time's pretty important with this one, tight margin and all that, as I'm sure you're aware, the money ring-fenced for this project could be put to good use elsewhere if there's any delay."

"Yes." Tom was aware, "I'm working on it." His jaw clenched.

"I'm sure you are." Arthur pressed a button and Carol came through, "Get these typed up properly would you, and take them downstairs, Miss Prempton. Ask them to get them drawn up straight away and copies out to the contractors. Thank you."

Carol nodded, blushed under Tom's scrutiny, took the rough-sheets and went back into the Annexe where she spent her working hours with the keyboard and photocopier. Tom leered after her retreating back and attempted to exchange a conspiratorial grin with Jim but found himself ignored. Arthur didn't offer a cup of coffee and they left soon afterwards.

Arthur decided to leave early. Carol came through to check the address of the Wild Rose Court project before going back in the Annexe.

The job was quite a 'good number', as Dorothy

called it, at least to begin with, although Carol had decided she wouldn't want to spend her life doing this. It was fine once you got the hang of it though, as a start.

It was typing, mostly, and writing out letters. Arthur would give a vague plan of what the letter should be about or start to dictate it. She would sit and write a beginning, cross it out then write down his next version after he had puzzled over it with much pursing of his lips, frowning at his feet or across the city, yellow in sunlight - then The Muse would suddenly descend and he would start again, confidently. "Dear Messrs, It has come to my notice, no, our alternative er, no, I am afraid we have been unable... yes that's it..." and then a whole sentence would be written out and half of the next then the city would get another hard stare.

Eventually and always, he'd sort of laugh, then scrawl down what he called 'the gist' of it on a scrap of paper and hand it to her with the request that she 'make it sound civilised' and send it off. But he'd always first go through the ritual of false starts and half-paragraphs.

It was a pile of such papers that she would come in to 'do' after a week or so of half- days when she took 'dictation', did the files, delivered reports and made coffee. There had used to be two secretaries on the section but now, with the 'climate' there was only the one. She was looking around for something else for when her contract was finished.

She typed out yesterday's plan-references. A note marked 'Urgent" had arrived by fax downstairs for Arthur.

She read it - she always read his mail. Arthur had asked her to sift the 'important bits'. She never knew which these were as it all seemed total nonsense so she would bring him an interesting selection, or ones with unusual stamps and put the rest in the bin.

It didn't seem to matter as he never knew which were important either and the whole process seemed to carry on regardless.

This note read, 'Arthur Pearce. Wild Rose Court: Unoccupied: For one day: 21st of this month: Reliable Source: T.H.'

What on earth was going on? Who was T.H.?

Wild Rose Court again - the plans were all there for whatever it was they were building. Arthur was no good to ask, he just thought you were being polite and turned the conversation, at the speed of light, to another discussion of Springer's latest antics. Carol wondered if those people she'd met were still living in their house at Wild Rose Court. She had meant to go back and thank them but never had, somehow. She had never told Dot about her weird adventure. Anna and Ralph. She remembered their names. She remembered the address from tracking it down on that awful night, trying to find sanctuary on her first night in London.

Perhaps she should call round there and see what was going on? She finished off the typing and then clocked out. Arthur was out, having coffee. She could make up the hours later in the week.

Chapter 16

It was much easier finding Wild Rose Court when you had money in your pocket, she noticed.

It was a cold, sunny afternoon and from the other end of the street she could see quite a crowd of people, all colours and sizes, in the narrow road between the two occupied houses. Some sitting, some standing. She felt suddenly self-conscious and wanted to turn back - with her stupid suit, patent shoes and ridiculous hair slide - but then she recognised Ralph standing at one of the gates and she carried on.

As she got closer she realised they were having a discussion about something. She stopped a short distance away and sat on a wall to listen. No one seemed to have noticed her.

"We'll just get our heads kicked in if we do that and for nothing..."

"Not if there's enough of us…"

"There isn't enough of us..."

"We could give as good as we get..."

"We shouldn't stoop to violence!" this voice stood

out - it was so clear and confident, Carol looked to see who it was. "We should remember our cause - let them drag us off to prison! Ours is a moral right! We will not defeat them with their own methods. We should be quite prepared to be jailed for our beliefs. Am I the only one who feels that way?"

No one answered. People looked at their feet. Apparently she was.

Anna was scathing. She had recognised the speaker. She had come along with Allan who was visiting his roots again.

"Yes, you're the only one who feels that way because you're the only one who can afford the fine! The rest of us would be inside."

People laughed. This was true.

"And this isn't a 'moral cause'," Anna continued, "it's just that we haven't got anywhere to live - so unless you're inviting us all round to your place I suggest you belt up."

Caroline looked deeply offended, Allan, standing next to her, looked deeply embarrassed.

"Either we go or we stay and fight. And then go. We wouldn't win in court and they'll have an army round here to clear us out sooner or later. I don't fancy that again. They could come at any time and they're not gentle..."

"They're coming on the 21st!"

Carol was surprised at how her voice sounded - all on its own among so many people. Faces turned to look at her and she felt herself redden.

"Hello, Carol," it was Anna. "What are you doing

here? What was that you said?"

Carol told them in a rush. "They're going to come on the 21st. They think this place is going to be empty on that day. I don't know why..."

People looked at each other as the date and its significance sank in.

"21st... the park festival's then... How did they know about that...? How did they know we'd all be going to that?"

"I work there. They got a message through. Today..."

"Who from?"

Speculation was fruitless.

Only Ralph guessed how they could have found out and swore under his breath.

The discussion continued.

"I still think we should go. I'd rather leave with some dignity than be dragged out by the hair."

"Then we may as well all just die with dignity, get it over with and cause no trouble at all."

"I think we could at least put up a fight. Give it a go. Especially if they won't be expecting it. How many are coming?"

"Why don't we get as many people down here as we can? Hold them off for at least one day. Then see what happens. I don't want to run out of here without at least having a go. What's the point?"

There was general agreement to this. Then it was put to a vote. No-one voted to leave without at least a protest. No-one voted to fight alone. Everyone voted to resist. Some hands went up straightaway and the others followed.

"Right, we get people here and standby to repel boarders."

People were smiling then, and feeling confident. They'd show 'em. If only for a day. People moved away to recruit support.

"Do you think there's any point?" said Reny.

"You never know. If we fight, we might win – if we don't fight – we'll definitely lose," remembered Anna. "Might as well organise something."

Ralph and Anna came over to talk to Carol.

"Fancy seeing you again? How did you find out about... Oh hello Allan."

"Hi there! Ralph told me what was happening. Caroline wanted to come and give her support."

"Everyone's welcome. You never know."

"No but we can all have a bloody good guess," muttered Anna.

Allan hovered uncertainly. "Anyhow, Carol, you were telling us how you found out about the 21st thingy..."

"Well, I work for them you see. That was that interview DCL Company - they're the ones who are going to - whatever it is they're going to do..."

"DCL?" queried Allan. "I thought that was clothes?"

"Some of it is I think, but the bit I work in is all

houses and things, flats and buildings."

Allan nodded at this. Anna was impatient with him asking irrelevant questions as if he knew anything about the world of high finance but he left at this point and went back to talk to Caroline - who was dressed down for the occasion, Anna noticed - wearing throw-offs from last season's collection. Whatever he told her seemed to shock Caroline, judging by the look on her face. She and Allan left soon afterwards.

They talked about the note that Arthur had received that very morning, telling when the houses would be empty, but couldn't figure out who could possibly have sent it. It was a complete mystery.

Ralph called a halt to the speculation as time-wasting. He sounded irritable. He knew exactly who had told them but couldn't bear for this to be known. Especially not by Anna.

They heard a description of the plans Carol had seen for the 'Development' but they didn't make much sense either.

The next few days were full of rain and busyness but the sun came out again for the 21st because it was special. A lot of strangers woke up in the rooms at Wild Rose Court and blinked out of sleeping bags or from under makeshift covers on all the floor space. All the residents had brought a friend plus someone.

"How the hell are we going to get tea for all this lot?" Ralph had queried.

"All been taken care of," he had been told, by Anna and Reny, "kind donation from Mo."

They had, in the kitchen, cardboard boxes of French-sticks and milk and tea-bags and other packets of purloined goodies.

"Not bloody pate again is it?"

People had to take turns with what cups and mugs there were but lives and souls would be kept together quite well.

There had been something of a party the night before and people awoke, bleary-eyed, collected something to eat or wandered about the house to look at the place and see who else had woken up.

Outside, the pale blue van moved into the court and crawled along it. The midday sun burned the windscreen into a golden blaze. Jim squinted into it and pointed out the two houses to the driver.

He hated his job sometimes. In fact, most of the time.

The pale blue van slowed to a halt at the kerb. They could see no movement in the house. It was empty - as they had been told it would be.

"Right, all out!" The foreman gave the orders. "There shouldn't be too much rough stuff, they're all away, or most. Do this side first."

The back doors were pushed open from the inside and the six men got out, lifting out large rectangles of wood and various tools for putting them in place across windows and doors.

Jim stayed in the van. He had to report back on the job done, but that didn't mean he had to take part in doing it.

They stood, flexing bulky arms and legs, and

looking up and down the street. All was quiet. Any ugly scenes would not be witnessed by the legally sleeping residents.

Jim was looking at the front door of the first house when it suddenly opened. A figure appeared, dressed in a manner which surprised him. She was carrying an organiser bag. Despite an unusually tousled look to the hairstyle, he recognised her before she had quite persuaded the door to close properly and turned to walk down the path.

Carol was following advice and getting out of the way early - no point in her risking her job. She had enjoyed the party though and was feeling unusually fragile in the bright sun.

Jim saw her face startle as she saw the van and the burly strangers leaning their boards against the garden wall. They looked at her with some surprise – the neat(ish) suit, the shoes, the bag - Jim realised he had shrunk back in his seat, though she didn't look into the van but turned quickly and disappeared back into the house.

The men looked at each other in surprise - Carol didn't look as if she ate babies on anything like a regular basis.

Carol raced up the stairs, her heart pounding, aware that she was afraid of what was about to happen.

"They're here!" she yelled as loudly as she could. "They're outside!"

Eyes were all suddenly wide-awake and she saw that she wasn't alone in being afraid.

"How many are there?"

"About... um..." Her mind raced and went blank. How many? A thousand? Fifty? No... "...About five. I think. No, six!"

She could feel her heart slowing as simple mathematics came back to her.

"Any police?"

"Didn't see any."

"Great! Right. Everybody out!"

Blankets, bags and rolled up 'pillows' fell ragged on the floor and feet stumbled into worn shoes and trainers and everyone tried to get down the stairs at the same time.

Outside, the men paused in their unloading as the door to the house opened and, not four-or-five pathetic looking wastrels, but dozens - or was it scores? - of street-hardened, vicious-looking types poured out along the little path, trampled down the unkempt patch of garden and stared at them over the little wall.

There was no shouting, no abuse, no heroes rushing forward desperately to be overwhelmed and dragged away, no helpless victims struggling pitifully against the kicks - just a solid wall of people, standing together, watching them. Waiting.

The men looked at each other, then at their chief, he hadn't prepared them for this. He closed his mouth and put down the toolbox he had been holding then put his hands in his pockets and stared at the rabble with venom in his eyes.

"You.... I..." it was a bad start because his voice

sounded small and weak in the chill air. He coughed. "You people!" he yelled as loud as he could, "You've no right to be here! You're breaking the law! Not get out quietly, we don't want any trouble!"

But it came out more like a request than an order. He had no muscle to enforce it and he knew it.

The silence when he had finished swallowed up the threat.

And there was still a crowd standing quietly and watching them, curiously.

"We don't want any trouble!" he repeated.

"So piss off then and you won't get any!" someone replied calmly.

The wall of people was smiling now - feeling the overwhelming strength of their numbers. It wasn't clear how it started but a ripple of movement traversed the crowd – they were each linking arms with the person next to them and now instead of individuals relying just on their own strength they were a wall, reinforcing each other's.

The six or seven men, looking a lot smaller than Carol remembered, shifted their stance and looked uneasy. What were they supposed to do against so many? They weren't paid to get done over by organised mobs. Quite the reverse was what they preferred.

"Sod this," murmured one, "I'm off. You coming?"

All except the chief went back to the van. He glared back and forth, opening and shutting his mouth, looking for the words that would inspire fire in his men and send them forward, over the top and out of the trench and forward in the face of overwhelming odds and onward ever onward - but he couldn't think of any.

Then he shrugged his shoulders up against the cold and walked back to the van.

"Can't you do anything?" he asked Jim, who was trying to keep from laughing.

"Like what?"

"They'll have to get the Old Bill on this one."

"Fair enough. Back to farm then."

Jim felt relieved as the van backed down the street. He could pick out a few faces who he recalled had been heckling Tom. They were standing there, in the ridiculously overgrown garden, shivering, expecting more trouble from the pale, alien van. They were supposed to be away today. The source must have got it wrong... then he remembered that girl who worked in Arthur's office.

How was she mixed up in this? Did she live there? A kind of double life? A weird entanglement? Had Arthur sent her to do some spying?

"Drop me off here," he said as soon as they had got far enough away not for it not to look suspicious. He was going to find out what was going on. The driver was looking at him, puzzled.

"We'll let you know when you can go in," said Jim, "you'll get your money for today anyway."

"Too right we will," said the chief and drove off. Jim started back towards Wild Rose Court.

They had all cheered as the van disappeared

around the corner, its blue smoke vanishing in seconds. People went over to the second, still-sleeping houseful to tell them they'd missed it.

"That's it then. They'll go to the courts now, then the pigs will be here."

"Well I won't be."

"Pity, I feel like having another go now. We saw them off, didn't we?"

There was some agreement to this. Victory - even a small one - tasted good.

"They wouldn't mess about though would they? And we don't know how many of them could come back."

"Where's the lovely Caroline today... speaking of numbers?" someone asked. "She was all for being hauled down the nick the other day - now she's not even here. Nor Allan."

"They left when they found out who was taking over the place. Her dad owns it."

"What shall we all do now then? How many want to stay on for the next round?"

Generally people wanted to get on and look for somewhere else to live without risking a run-in with the law. At least they had bought more time and seen off the enemy for once - or at least a small, scouting force of the enemy.

Ralph suddenly cleared his throat, got up on the garden wall and made a little speech to the crowd of friends, thanking everyone there for turning up, for the party and for seeing off the troublemakers for at least one day.

"And when this place where now I stand is but a car-park, and when our poor dear rhododendron is no more..." A long 'Aah' greeted this and Ralph put his hand on his heart. "I hope they will put up a plaque to the Brave Battle fought this day - as an inspiration to those that come after..." People started applauding and cheering. "We will fight them in our workplaces, we will fight them in the mines, we'll do battle in the streets and in schoolyards, but today..." People were clapping and cheering... "we fought them in Our Beautiful Garden... and, what is more... We won!"

He was drowned out in applause.

Anna and Carol were still clapping when he came over and they went back in the house to pick up what they could take with them. They would only have a few more days at the most. And it wouldn't be wise to be around when they came back with their allies.

Reny came with them, and Mike, who had arrived in time for the party, and the Battle - only to find there was nowhere for him and Reny to live and that they would be moving on again soon. Carol decided she was going to be 'ill' that day and helped to look through cupboards for things useful and portable.

"Hello? Is anyone there?" the unfamiliar voice came floating up the stairs. They went quickly to look but Jim was already on the landing.

"They're back."

"No they're not, it's just me! Can I come in?"

They recognised him and didn't know what to say. Reny did.

"What do you think you're doing here. Fuck off out of it while you can!"

"Come off it, son, I've come for a pow-wow."

"Who are you calling 'son'?"

"Just an expression." Jim suddenly remembered hating it when people had used to call him 'son'.

Halcyon days.

"You're one of the bastards who're throwing us out and you were round here measuring."

"Well not really," Jim hesitated, maybe he shouldn't have come... "I was doing my job, like I have to, that's all."

Reny snarled, "So was Goebbels."

"I'm looking for someone actually - she was here this morning... works at the same place I do..." Jim looked around, Carol wasn't much in evidence at that point. "Know who I mean?"

Nobody, it seemed, had a clue.

"Well if you see her, tell her I just wanted to know what was going on. I don't like this sort of business either." He glanced at Reny, who just glared back. "I got into this line to build houses for people - not knock 'em down."

"Are you apologising?" Reny sneered.

"Maybe. What else can I do?"

"Get your pals to refuse to chuck us out?"

"I don't think I could do that."

"Piss off, then, you're wasting our time."

Carol emerged at this point from where she had ducked to hide as soon as she had recognised Jim.

"You won't tell them I was here will you?"

"Same to you. Just wanted to know if there was anything..." his voice faded. There wasn't anything he could do, of course, and he shouldn't have bothered.

"What are they going to do with the site, do you know?" Anna asked as she led the way into the living room. They may as well offer hospitality while they had it to offer. "Anything exciting? Nightclub? Nuclear dump? Dole-office?"

"Oh no, nothing like that," Jim dug in his jacket pocket.

"Children's home? Old people's centre?" the suggestions came, but Jim kept shaking his head and digging in various pockets. Eventually, he pulled out a folded piece of paper and opened it out onto the floor.

It was a plan of the whole street with the last two houses – theirs - mapped out – this one was just coloured in grey but Liz's house was mapped out in detail of its inner shapes with 3-figure numbers all over the place - mapped out in layers in eye-boggling detail.

"No, nothing like that," said Jim. "Your, er, this house, is going to get knocked down. That's what the grey means."

"Knocked down? Why?"

Jim shrugged. "Market's tight," he said, "they only need one lot. Can't sell more than that. Not quick enough anyway. Fast returns see. That other house will be really up-market flats. All the best. All this part where we are now will be a lovely green area with trees and everything I expect, nice open space... Oh sorry." He realised he wasn't being diplomatic. "You see your place, if you'll forgive the jargon, is knackered. At least more knackered than the other one. And they only want one. So... you're knackered."

He looked up from the diagrams.

"Bastards!" said Reny. It seemed all there was to say.

"They're bastards alright, know that for sure," Jim said with feeling. "If that's any comfort. But I don't suppose it is."

Ralph was still looking at the plan.

A question occurred to him.

About an hour later the group was still discussing the answer - and all the other questions it had brought with it, when Mike came running up the stairs, eyes wide.

"You should see what's coming down the street! You'd better get out!"

They went outside. It was a huge transporter, carrying a squatting, yellow-muscled bulldozer-type machine with an arm like a crane but with a weight and chain. They watched the huge formation come towards them. The driver, tiny next to the machines got out of the cabin and came up to them. The engine noise cut out leaving a buzzing noise in their ears.

"What's going on?" asked the driver. "Aren't they done yet?"

"Still occupied," said Jim, "cock up at head-office."

The driver swore. "They might have told me. What am I supposed to do with this?"

They all had suggestions but none of them were polite so they kept quiet and looked puzzled as if trying to help with the problem.

"We'll be in touch as soon as the place is cleared," said Jim.

"Well my boss will be in touch. This messes up the schedules. Ah well. Not my worry. You people live here?"

They nodded.

"Shame, nice place," the driver looked up at the house, then got back in the cabin, closed the door, started up the engine and began the long slow reverse out of the street.

"Now do you believe me?" said Jim. "They don't use those things for doing a bit of decorating. It'll take a couple of days to get the law down here. That's how long we've got."

"Right. Do we all know what we're doing?"

They all nodded.

"What are you doing, Reny?"

He was writing something down on his arm, glancing up at the transporter. He grinned at them.

"Nothing. Good luck with your plan. We'll see you later."

Reny and Mike went back over to their place. Jim and Carol went off to catch buses home.

Ralph and Anna had a couple of days to get ready.

They would have to go around and see Allan that night and just hope that Caroline was out.

First, Anna hunted up some scissors and went over to see Liz.

Chapter 17

The dark, spectacled executive, with his elbow on the window sill and manicured hand on the leather-bound wheel, eyed the class-piece sauntering across the traffic-snarled, smoke-choked road with her lounge-lizard in tow.

That strange shade of jade did it - toning beautifully with the colour of her skin, in the silk T-dress under the huge, beautifully-cut coat-jacket, the designer sandals in the same eye-drawing shade. The poise, the easy swing of the walk, and, most of all, the look - the almost no-smile, catlike, doing-the-world-a-favour-by-being-on-it look. He loved it.

She saw, and merely accepted, his admiring stare as merely one among a myriad from a captivated world: lucky world! That was something. That was class. And dressed in silk.

The partner was an inferior creature - though obviously in the bread too, in spite of the, yes, slightly worried expression. Maybe she'd just told him to get off. Or maybe some of his shares had crashed. Had to be Somebody to be with a piece of ass like that.

The executive couldn't overhear the conversation as the well-heeled couple went past.

Anna was doing the talking.

"Look, it's easy. Just remember you own the place, the world owes you a living and everyone you meet is your congenital inferior!"

"I can't." Ralph felt conspicuous in the hand-made suit and shoes. The suit fitted okay but the leather brogues pinched.

"Well it is a bit tricky - you really need twelve years at a school where they teach you these things and then it all comes naturally. This is a crash course - so concentrate!"

"I feel like a complete pillock."

"Good, we're halfway there - all you 've got to do is start acting like one and we're home and dry."

"I can't talk like that."

"You don't talk, you whinny. Anyway, I'm doing the talking."

"We'll never get away with it."

"That's what they told Cromwell."

"It's also what they told Spartacus."

"Well, one out of two isn't bad. And who would have heard of Spartacus if he'd never given it a go?"

"It was easy for him - he had an army with him..."

"Well there isn't one handy. Just try to imagine that your great-great-great-great ever-so-great grandaddy was a bootlicker, and a dab hand at the old rape-and-pillage routine back in the days of Yore."

"Your what?"

"Your grandaddy."

"What the hell's that got to do with it?"

"I don't know - I'm not making the laws, I'm just breaking 'em, but you'd probably own half of Scotland by now if he had been, so just try and imagine he was. And you do. Go on."

Ralph tried. A more assertive, self-assured look came onto his face and rested there.

"My grandaddy was a pillock!" he said proudly to an alarmed passer-by.

"That's the idea, now you're getting it," Anna approved.

Ralph preened, revelling in his new -found heritage and gene-bank. He smirked at the world obnoxiously.

"That's great!" said Anna. "Now just hold that."

They crossed another street and then were looking up at the glass and concrete and glass and more concrete towering hulk of DCL Ltd.

"You could have fooled me," muttered Ralph, unnerved, despite his pillaging ancestors, and gazing up at the monolith which hung over him.

"Relax will you, it's only a building," Anna was in her element and was just waiting for the curtain-call and cue - but she was a little worried by the quality of the supporting cast whose teeth were chattering.

"All we're doing is popping in to see 'Daddykins', who's in conference today and tell him about my little engagement, honey."

She blew Ralph a kiss.

"We don't even know he'll be there. They don't clock in you know."

"What did Carol say - top-shareholder's meeting today, he'll be there. Top-floor suite. Relax. Come on, look elegant, sophisticated and confident. And rich."

Ralph sniffed and dragged his hand-made sleeve across his nose, "If you insist."

Anna took his arm and marched him down towards the steps, slowing as they neared.

Ralph sensed Anna go away somewhere he could not follow. He looked at her. There was a stranger walking by his side. She moved differently, her face held on display to the world. Her eyes looked out from under slightly lowered lids behind the designer shades, her head tilted slightly back. He looked away and wished Anna were there.

She stopped at the foot of the white steps which led up to DCL's front-doors, ran a long-nailed hand through her new, slick, hairstyle - Liz's own contribution to the proceedings - and gazed up complacently at the heaviness of power ahead of them. She stood as if conversing with Ralph and told him what she could see. It corresponded with Carol's description.

"Only two guards on, no one else about, come on."

Ralph urgently wanted to go home. This was madness. They were going to get caught and have horrid things done to them. Probably by horrid people in sunglasses. But the stranger had started up the steps and turned back to him, laughing, saying,

"Well that's what I told him anyway," in a voice of trained sophistication he had only heard from Caroline before.

He was compelled to follow in support, up the steps, his arm linked with the laughing stranger's.

"So if Daddy's not here we'll just leave a little message," she continued happily as they neared the doors.

But he couldn't listen. His back was cold with sweat. They were within earshot of the guards. Ralph bent his head as if to listen to the bubbling, lilting flow of twaddle from his partner and looked at the guards from under his brows.

They were watching and made some private comment or other. Ralph looked down at his feet, took a deep breath and swallowed.

Anna finished what she had been saying as they reached the door. Ralph risked a look at her. She paused at the top of the steps and looked around her. She looked completely relaxed and at ease, as if she was enjoying herself immensely. She saw him looking and smiled at him. Anna was still there. He tried to smile back.

One of the guards was holding the door open and carefully scrutinising this dangerous looking woman. He got showered with a smile-full of grace and stared. Ralph went in after her but no-one seemed to notice. Anna glided over to the reception desk. The woman's hand appeared automatically, reaching up for the tag or the ID - neither of which they had. But Anna didn't seem to have noticed the hand.

"Please could you tell me where Daddy is? Oh

sorry, I mean Adam Singleton. Mr Singleton. He's in one of his silly meetings today, poor darling, do you know which floor that is?"

They had calculated on the fact that debutantes rarely got presented to receptionists.

The woman looked up from the telephone, irritated at first, then flustered as she realised who the 'poor darling' must be. Anna used the advantage, her voice soft and clear, perfectly audible all over the foyer.

"Could you just let him know we're on the way up?"

"He's... but... Mr Singleton's in conference at the moment... with Mr Carmichael. Have you any ID... er... please?"

She clung to crumbling routine under fire.

Anna flung her a conspiratorial smile.

"Oh he won't mind, not when we tell him..." she laid her strangely be-jewelled hand elegantly on Ralph's arm. The woman's eyes followed Anna's and came to rest on the huge glittering rock on Anna's third finger.

"You see, we've got a little announcement... and Daddy wouldn't like to get it over the Tannoy... and I do so want to tell him before the papers get hold of it - you know what an old softie he is..."

The receptionist didn't know, nor did Anna, but who was to say?

"We're going to tell Paul's family tonight after the ball, isn't it wild?" She stopped and radiated up at Ralph - who tried to look as if he had been weaned on banquets and bought diamonds as big as eggs most days of the week, while hoping to God the wet patches he could feel under his arms were not showing.

The receptionist was utterly charmed. Anna had overstepped proprietary and confided in her by exactly the right amount. Her eyes were on the hunk of diamond (found in a corner of Caroline's top-drawer during yesterday's rummage, with Allan panicking at the door that she would return early and Ralph telling him to either belt-up or be filled-in) which was on Anna's third finger, and her mind fabricated its very own Girls' Own paperback in a daze of sentiment. The everyday dross fell away and was replaced by a vision of the kind of life she would only ever know through fiction. Anna looked back at her - the enraptured heroine on the arm of a young God after dizzying, deadly adventures and on the wild threshold of the promises of life. The receptionist flushed and her face, grim, careworn and overworked, melted into a smile and tears winked behind the horn-rims as bright youth was re-called.

She reached over, almost without knowing it, and ran up a couple of guest tags, ahead of Miss Anastasia Singleton, but not for long, and Mr Paul Nigel Horton-Smythe, smiled Anna as the woman tapped into the machine.

As she took the tags, the woman took her hand and whispered, "And may I say, I hope you will be very happy. He's on the top floor. The lift's in there." They had counted on receptionists not knowing directors or their families well. Or if Singleton even had a daughter.

Anna thanked her and beamed at Ralph as he took his tag, he felt sick – but Anna took his hand and did 'the young shepherdess with her swain' all the way down to the lift for the benefit of any who cared to watch - and most did.

Ralph felt it was laying it on a bit strong. But then decided he didn't mind.

The lift arrived and they stepped inside, the door hushed closed and they rose up into the building.

Anna collapsed against the wall, eyes closed and breathed out. She crossed her arms and forced a shiver to get rid of the trembling that had started to threaten.

"I nearly got my name wrong! Shit!"

But then they were at the floor where Carol worked. Ralph checked the watch he was wearing. They were just about on time.

"Come on, you're doing marvellous." He took her hand. Outside there were a million miles of corridor. They walked down them, ID tags held conspicuously. Fifth, no, fourth door on the right. Just on time. There. Open

Maybe he'd returned early... maybe not left yet... but the office was empty except for Carol who stared at them as if they were the last people she expected to see. She pulled them into the room, "I thought you weren't coming! Quick, in here."

They hardly saw Arthur's main office as they ran across it into the Annexe with things crawling up their backs telling them that Arthur would return before they got across the floor. In the annexe, the new computer had arrived and was waiting to be installed into the rest of the system in the building. They ducked behind its bulk next to the window.

Anyone coming into the little room would have to walk around the machine to see them. They shifted about to get comfortable on the floor.

"What if he comes in to look in the filing cabinet?"

"He won't, he doesn't understand it, now hush!"

Carol wiped her top lip with a tissue and slipped back behind her desk just in case he did come in on return from lunch. She did not look at the computer or think about the two hiding behind it. They did not exist - or she would never get through this afternoon. Something was bound to go wrong.

She got out a letter and started to decode it.

In their hideaway, they stretched their legs out to the wall under the window and leaned back, looking up at the small strip of sky they could see above the wall. Ralph thought of something and he turned to whisper to Anna.

"A minute if you will, please Carol!" - loud and horribly close, it made them both jump. They heard Carol's chair scrape back, her steps across the floor and her bright, innocent, "Yes sir? A letter is it?" and the door closing behind her. They breathed out.

They sat listening to Arthur's attempts at composition. They stared at the sky, easing themselves in silent agony as bits of them went into cramp or numbness or one leant too hard on the other. Anna unwittingly dug a long false nail into Ralph's thigh whilst trying to balance herself when easing off the agonising shoes. His silent, wild-eyed grimace of pain threw her into a giggling fit and he fell in after: for what seemed hours they were in that kind of ecstatic hell where laughter roars in the mind and throat and stomach but must not be let out and so builds, swells and hammers to be released. Out of the sea of fear and strained nerves came waves of laughter which they could only hold back by thinking of what might happen if they and Carol were found out.

When it had passed, Ralph got a pen out of Allan's jacket pocket, slipped a sheet of paper off the top of the pile on the computer, wrote down a question and passed it to Anna. She thought for a while, let him read her answer, then wrote her own question for him.

Their shadow, on the wall and on the computer, moved slowly round as the afternoon passed.

Chapter 18

Reny wished he had not turned up so early. There was so long to wait and nothing to do. His hands were red with cold. There were no dogs anyway - that was what had worried him most. Rottweilers didn't make good company.

From what he could see inside the yard there was only a small, shabby looking office. It had a phone in it and someone sat at a desk. Twice while they had been there, taking it in turns between this bus-stop, which was opposite the main gate, and the cafe down the road - the wooden gates had opened and a truck one time and an ordinary van the next, had pulled out and driven off. Now all seemed quiet. They could have no idea how many people might be inside the compound but it would be unlikely to be more than a couple.

It looked as if all the heavy-duty business vehicles were parked inside a long, dull-looking building with small, dirt-curtained windows and sliding, sectioned doors. Reny was familiar with the type. The whole of the compound was surrounded by a wooden fence on top of a red-brick wall.

The top of the fence was jagged and topped with barbed-wire.

None of it was designed to look inviting.

They had double-checked the address he had copied down from the visiting 'dozer. This was the right place.

Reny went back to the café. It was on the same main road. Mike was sitting over the second cup of tea they had invested in to justify their presence. Skin had formed on it.

It was a big transport cafe as they were near the motorway. They sat among plastic trays and plastic plants and looked for hazards in the plan. There were dozens.

An ironic wolf-whistle greeted Reny's plumage.

"What if we get sent down?"

"At least we'll have a roof over our heads. And at least we won't get on each other's nerves. Anyway, they can't send you down for trespass."

"Even if they do, I want to have a go at the bastards first. I've about had it with being pushed around. Want another tea?"

"No thanks, I'm still looking at this one."

"I didn't think you'd have me doing a job my first week away from home."

"You've always underestimated me." He touched Mike's arm, briefly, which was the nearest he dared get to a show of affection in the atmosphere of that place. "Don't worry, we'll get this finished with before you know it. If there's any danger, we'll just forget it and go home."

"We haven't got one."

"OK, Plan B - if there's any danger you deal with it and I'll meet you back here."

"Fine. This is the right place, isn't it?"

"You've got real faith in me, haven't you?"

"Born to follow."

"Do you want to go and see if anything's happening?"

Mike groaned, took the gloves they were sharing, and left.

The tea-time rush came in. Most people looked at Reny's war plume and sat elsewhere. He liked that.

*

Dusk was setting in early.

"Bye-bye, see you tomorrow, Carol," Arthur put his head round the door amiably, nearly giving Ralph heart failure. "You alright? Look a bit peaky?"

"No, I'm fine, just a bit tired," said Carol, trying to look relaxed but looking manic instead.

"All these late nights, I don't know – you youngsters. Well, I'll leave you to it."

He went out and they heard the outer office door close. Ralph and Anna groaned out loud with relief and dared to stretch out their aching limbs. Carol came around to them, speaking in a stage whisper, "Don't come out yet, he sometimes forgets things." They appealed to her, silently, from pins-and needles and cramp and numbness. "Just a bit longer," she insisted.

She looked down out of the window and waited until the much-diminished figure of Arthur - more rotund from a bird's-eye view - emerged from under the window-ledge and rolled on invisible legs across the car park.

His was not one of the super-sleek autos which had been parked in the front row - and now long gone home.

His faithful old Jag awaited in the fourth row back: the sanctuary at the end of the day to carry him through the insanity of the rush-hour's beginning, out of the smoke and dust and rush out onto the flyover which swept over the worst and into quiet suburbs where quiet people lived out their quiet lives. He wouldn't go straight back there tonight though. Clara was out and wouldn't be back until late. There was a pleasant little restaurant he knew of where they did a good glass of wine and where you could sit and look out at the river. It would make a pleasant supper.

Better than the big, empty house anyway.

"Right, he's gone."

They tried to spring to their feet but nature had had other ideas in their design than their crouching behind computers for hours and they were only able to rise up, sedately, wincing and groaning.

"Some urban guerrillas we are. The rheumatic-paratroopers or what?"

They wandered round the annexe like bears waking up in Spring, stretching and rubbing to get the blood going again. Carol watched, trying not to see the funny side at their expense. She fetched an over-sized stiff, brown envelope from the cabinet.

"This is it. Jim kept it back for me. Everything's down there that you need."

Ralph took the envelope, "I dunno, my first job as a draughty and I won't even get paid." He pulled out the thin blue sheet of paper to check it. "Okay, lead the way."

"Jim'll be able to get it back there tomorrow and no one will notice. Come on." Carol led the way after checking the corridor. "All clear," she breathed, "but you'll have to be quiet, there's someone working late in the next office."

Their steps were loud and echo-y on the lino. They took the stairs as it was quieter and safer than the lift. A light was on in one of the rooms next to the one they wanted. Carol unlocked the door and gave them the key to lock themselves in. She didn't speak but crossed her fingers for them. Anna blew her a kiss in reply, then eased the door handle down, closed the door so very quietly and released the handle, hands sticky.

They breathed more easily when Anna had put the key in the lock and eased it round, tense until the sharp click as the bolt shot home. They waited, convinced that the worker next door, the guards downstairs and the people already at home and watching telly had heard that click, but no one came running to hammer down the door and haul them away, so they breathed again. They looked round the room.

All the tables seemed to have been up-ended - the edges of all the drawing-boards jutted up into the half-darkness. They moved around. Ralph found the drawing gear he needed to supplement his own that he had brought along. Jim had put in several sheets spare to allow for false starts. Ralph found a table out of the way of the door and switched on one of the small table lamps.

The brightness scalded his eyes temporarily. Then he set to work, his head moving from one plan to the other, newly forming, his hands, the T-square and the pens making a quiet hush across the paper.

Anna, feeling redundant, wandered about looking at the half-finished plans and diagrams and smiling at the very-well finished doodles drawn lovingly on edges of the boards. She thought she recognised a caricature of Tom, unkindly accurate and doing something quite rude.

She walked into a stool and only just caught it and decided it was safer to sit.

She decided to pass the time by drawing Ralph. After a third attempt, when he still looked like a frog, squatting on a wall, she gave it up and looked out of the window.

All was grey mist, speckled with lights of white, red and orange like an electric galaxy. It was fascinating. For about ten-seconds flat.

She looked over at Ralph, completely engrossed in the circle of white light. While she watched, he swore angrily, under his breath, screwed up the piece of paper and started again on another. No room for conversation there.

The clock told her about ten-minutes had passed. She wished she'd brought along a little light reading. Like Das Kapital, Volume One. The clock ticked on.

The drawing started taking shape.

*

They had found the right place. It was eight o'clock. The cars were just loud noises with white lights swinging to red as they swept past in the darkness. The barbed wire was silhouetted, prettily, against the navy sky. Reny looked at it anxiously.

"Don't worry," said Mike, "You'll get over that easy. Try it with your eyes closed just to make it interesting!"

"Great – I'm already gay and Asian and now you want me to be disabled as well?"

"Guess I'm just kinky that way."

"And I'd never know which workshop to go to!"

They waited.

An elderly man had appeared around the curve in the road. He was leading a white Jack-Russell on a lead. It snuffled at the bottom of the wall and lifted its leg. The man clicked at it and said something Reny and Mike couldn't hear. They were both trying to look nonchalant and inconspicuous, as if standing on the edge of a road outside a closed compound at night was the in-thing to do.

The man shambled past, warily, with his dog, stiff-legged and ratty-looking, and dwindled into the night.

Reny nodded and Mike went to the edge of the curve and looked along the road in that direction while Reny did the other. He found himself willing someone - anyone - to appear and delay it again but the road spun away empty into the distant mess of lights.

He turned and signalled 'all clear'. Mike did the same. They ran to the spot they'd selected. Mike cupped his hands, Reny stepped onto them and up onto the wall, grabbing for the top edge of the fence. Mike passed up the brand-new wire-cutters - an unintended free gift from the do-it-yourself/help yourself super-store.

Reny cut through the two strands of wire, close to the uprights and pushed them away from him. He edged along the wall down to the next upright and cut there. The sections fell into space beyond the wall, making a singing sound as they fell. He was glad it hadn't been in coils - you never knew where they were going to flail when cut.

He closed the cutters, dropped them into his jacket pocket and reached down for Mike.

Mike got up on the wall then went straight on up, one foot in Reny's hand, onto the wooden palisade, feet scrabbling for a hold, balanced for a second laying flat out along the top of the fence to look down into the black vacuum beyond. Then he rolled over, let go and fell.

Reny heard him land, on his feet - like a cat would have done.

"Okay, come on," came the whispered call.

It's alright for the agile of this world, Reny thought.

He gripped the rough, sharp edges of the fencing and pulled, his feet trying to get a grip in their worn trainers. Then they held against the wooden strips and he was up. For an awful moment he felt he was going over head first into the void but held on, the top of the fence cutting into his chest, until he had got his legs up level and then over and down he went, almost before he could balance, landing badly.

"You OK?"

Reny stamped around for a bit to check his foot wasn't done in and nodded. They looked around them and listened. There was a light on, still, in the office over by the gate. That was all.

They kept in the deepest dark under the wall and walked quickly to where the vehicles should be, every nerve on the jump for a shout or a bark. Mike knew he had seen too many war -movies when he realised he was keeping an eye-out for the searchlight and the Tower. He didn't say anything about this but wished the images of machine-guns would go away. They got to the garage and opened their jackets, pulling out two plastic bags which were suspended from straps around their necks so they could be carried whilst leaving their hands free.

Reny got his knife out and ran the biggest blade down the edge of the door until he hit the lock. For a while he thought it wasn't going to go - bits of wood gave way and paint flaked off, then it caught. The door opened with a sigh.

He caught it and looked back to the light in the shed but could see no movement.

"C'mon."

Inside was pitch black and they could hardly see each other never mind anything else.

"Is it in here?"

"Must be, 's'not outside."

They moved warily into the blackness. The key-fob light they had was almost useless but just enough to see metal surfaces when they got close. There was a heavy smell of dirt and oil and petrol fumes. Mike's hand made contact with a metal edge. It was a bumper. They groped their way around the truck, a very faint sheen on its front, then onward into the darkness. The trucks all seemed to be parked at the same angle, probably in marked out spaces which they couldn't see. There were four of them. Then they were walking into an empty space.

Reny thought he could make out a shape to their left and they moved towards it. It was closer than they thought and their outstretched hands came suddenly to rest on a jointed, wide-ridged surface, flat under their touch and rough with dried mud. Caterpillar tracks. Mike risked a glimpse with the small torch.

"This is it!"

They tried to figure out which way it was pointing but it had a canvas cover on over its top part. They had to fumble about for an age to get it off. Mike found the Industrial Velcro-like fastening-strip and pulled it open with a deep, ripping sound. After that it pulled away easily. Reny took the wire cutter and climbed into the cabin. It only took a few minutes.

He had always loved mechanics.

While he was busy, Mike found the petrol cap - an irregular bump on the smooth metal body. He unscrewed it. Both the plastic bags were emptied into the tank.

"Lovely. Now just add two eggs, stir and pop in the oven for about two weeks," Reny imitated Mo giving a recipe.

"Big oven!" muttered Mike.

"Where's the bloody petrol cap? We don't want them to see it's been done."

They scrabbled around in the dark until Mike found it safe in his pocket. They screwed the petrol cap back on, feeling jumpy. The night watchman might be doing a round at any time.

But there was another 'dozer next to the first.

"Shit! Didn't think there'd be two!" Reny did the same again, cutting the wires but that wasn't certain enough.

"I didn't bring enough mix for two Oh, I know..."

They used the wire-cutters and their hands to scratch and dig up handfuls of earth from the hard-packed floor, scooping it up and dropping it as neatly as they could into the second petrol tank until it seemed to be enough.

"Great. Even if they fix the wires, the engines will crank up on that stuff. They won't get 'em going again in a hurry."

They couldn't risk the time it would take to get the covers back on which would have delayed their work being found out until the machines were needed, but they couldn't help that.

They got to the door. That would have to be left swinging open as well. Reny pushed it shut and jammed a piece of flotsam off the floor under it to hold it closed. It was the best they could do to disguise their visit.

Back at the wall there a sheer fifteen foot climb back out - the fencing was flush to the wall on this side and there was not a handhold anywhere. Their breath was steam in the night air.

"It'll have to be the gate."

It had wooden crossbeams on the inside.

"Right, it'll have to be a run, jump, one foot on that, grab for the top and over. There's no barbed wire."

'No barbed-wire!' thought Mike, looking at the tall, spiked wooden gates, great, let's party! But he said nothing.

They gave themselves a long enough run-up. The light from the shed fell in two oblongs on the dirt-ground. They could see a man inside, drinking tea from a big mug. Between gulps he seemed to be talking to himself, or to the floor. While they watched, he broke a biscuit and dropped half on the floor.

It was like watching someone on the telly - the little box of the window was brightly lit and he was oblivious of them watching.

"If we don't make it, there's only one of him, right?" Reny nodded, and made up his mind to get over that gate.

They took a good look first, making sure where the crossbar was. Mike took the left half, Reny the right.

They were across the gap, the sound of their trainers loud on the ground and the gate filled all the sky in seconds, the cross-bar lost in the dark-shape. Reny launched himself at the gate; his foot found the beam and pushed him up. The gate shuddered and banged with the impact.

He caught the top of the gate and pulled himself up. Mike was thrown back, missing the cross-bar, the shed door opened, a dog barked and the man shouted at it to, "Seek!"

Mike ran back a little way and took another run. Reny, one leg over the top of the gate, reached down to grab Mike's hands and pull him up. As Mike came up off the ground, Reny found himself looking down into the snarling red mouth and black eyes of the dog that was leaping up after him.

But the dog fell back, with its mouth empty, and started an ear-splitting racket. The man had gone back inside and was probably ringing the police.

Reny kept hold of Mike until they were both over the gate, back down on the pavement and running. The dog threw itself in frenzy at the gate. It rattled and swung against the lock - but it held - and the barking carried on as they ran.

They stopped down a side-street, after putting as many twists and turns between them and the compound as they could while still able to breathe. Their lungs hurt. "We're going to have to quit smoking."

"We're going to have to quit getting chased by bloody great dogs, you mean."

"You're right - that's what I mean. Where did that thing come from?"

"I was going to commend you on your surveillance of the place, but I won't. He must have had it with him in his shed some company!"

"And what's funny?"

Mike was laughing. He stopped, still trying to get his breath, "Your face when you jumped into that place!"

"You're face jumping out!" They both laughed.

Their breathing returned to normal.

"I don't want to have to do that again for a while."

"Aw! Don't say that - it was the cheapest date I could find!"

Reny put his arms around Mike and held him close.

"Boring sod. Never take me anywhere exciting." He kissed him.

"Where are we sleeping tonight?"

"Hm, wasn't actually planning on much sleep tonight. Haven't seen you for a while. Don't know. I'll meet you at the Bell. About half an hour. They'll be looking for two - if he saw us at all. I'd better get another hair cut - we'd better split up."

"Not just yet though."

After a while they went off in different directions, one took the wire-cutters to get rid of on the way and the other the plastic bags.

Chapter 19

The second draft had also ended up in the bin. Ralph's training was rustier than he had thought and he was starting to worry. Then Anna gave the signal that it was 'cleaner time'.

They left the room, checking the corridor was empty. The late-night worker next-door had left some time ago. They went up to the next floor as Carol had told them. The cleaners worked through the building in a kind of zigzag. Each team did two floors alternately, working along one and up the stairs at the far end then back along the second floor, up two flights and start again. They started at 8:30 and the team would be due on their floor around nine. All Ralph and Anna had to do was get out of the way and stay ahead of them, going back downstairs when the cleaners had gone on up.

No lights were on now and they wandered about until they heard voices on the next floor and then sat in one of the windows, looking out at the city. It was bitter cold now the heating was off. They took it in turns with Caroline's coat and then shared it. The voices and the noise of buckets against mops came suddenly loud from their right and they crept down the stairs again, taking care that all the cleaners had gone on up the other way.

The room now smelt tangy with disinfectant and the floor was slippy. Anna locked the door again and Ralph got back to the drawing. They took it in turns to wear the coat. Anna had filled a bin with paper doilies and lines of paper-dolls she had torn out of graph paper. She took a peek at Ralph's work:

It was like a mirror image of the original - one house was dissected in every detail - the other like a shadow, merely outlined. They heard the cleaners head down to the lifts and home, still discussing something. The night went on and the plan was gradually and carefully finished. Ralph's back and eyes ached.

There was nothing else to do except put it in the right place for the morning, make sure there were no stray copies of the original left lying about, go back up to the office, let themselves back in with Carol's key and try and get some sleep on the floor of the little annexe until morning.

Caroline's coat was treated to more abuse. They had to abandon their feet to freeze and resting on the hard floor in the cramped space meant having to move too often to sleep. Giving it up as a bad job they started talking, just generally at first, to pass the time. They ended up sitting with their knees up and huddled under the coat against the cold, backs against the computer and talking until they fell asleep - head-on-head-on-shoulder.

That was how Carol found them the next morning when she came in.

She told them the bad news.

"They've contacted the demolition contractor already and they're going in TODAY so we can't get the new plan to them in time. We can't stop them. They'll go ahead with the old one - they've already got that. I'm so sorry."

The new 'plan' waited in the drawer, but it would never be used.

Carol had brought them coats from home to put on. They waited until a reasonable hour when there were plenty of people about and left, Anna dressed in Carol's coat, with no makeup and the designer gear stuffed in a plastic bag. No one gave them a second glance as they left the building. They got to the bottom of the steps.

It had all been for nothing.

They spent the rest of the day at Allan's, or rather at Caroline's. She was away for a few days and Allan was packing.

"Where you going?"

"Don't know." He shrugged, "It's over."

"Oh?" Ralph tried to look surprised.

"We just reached rock-bottom, I suppose. She met someone else," Allan looked really dejected. "A biker," he said to Ralph's questioning face.

Ralph felt a pang of sympathy. There wasn't much down for him either really. Caroline had liked him as a piece of rough but he'd become domesticated since moving in with her.

"Thanks for your help in this one anyway, mate.

Something'll crop up," said Ralph.

Allan went out.

"Poor sod," Ralph muttered.

"Huh," said Anna, not at all moved by the spectacle.

She had decided to have a bath in the turquoise-tiled and deep-carpeted bathroom. She poured in a rainbow of coloured fragrant oils which promised to do various wonderful things to skin, hair, feet and various other bits, and lay back in the scented, bubbled heat.

Ralph discovered a drinks cabinet and raided it. There was a book on cocktails and he mixed something pale blue and spicy, delivered an order for one around the bathroom door and kept another on hand in the kitchen.

He opened the larder and paused for a moment, impressed. "They must have been expecting us! Us and everybody else."

He got out some pans, raided the fridge, calculated a common denominator which would include as many of the discoveries as possible and got on with it, sipping a deep green-concoction now and again and slipping refills around the door of the bathroom as required.

When Allan got back, Ralph was cooking, looking very happy, and there was singing coming from the bathroom.

"She'll be back by tomorrow," he said nervously. "You'd better be gone by then."

"Don't worry; we won't give her any cause for

complaint."

"Wouldn't hear it anyway, mate, not where I'm going." He sounded more sure of himself than he had done earlier.

"Oh?" Ralph was hoping to hear more but Allan was tapping on the bathroom door.

"Anna? Can I come in?"

"You may! Is there any more ice?" Ralph heard as the door closed.

Anna was wrapped in a jade towel and was just finishing off varnishing her toenails purple. The tortoiseshell cabinet had been opened and its contents thoroughly rifled.

"Oh, hello Allan. How's life?" Anna sipped from her glass. She could get used to this, she had decided.

"Anna, can we have a chat for a minute?" Allan closed the door. "Ralph told me you'd be going up north for a while after this house thing's over and - well I was wondering... this thing with Caroline... I think you were right and... well we all make mistakes you know."

He sat down on the turquoise carpet and looked sheepish.

He had always rather liked that expression on himself; it suited him and looked very appealing.

Anna went on varnishing her nails.

He went on, "I think things went wrong with you and me with all the trouble with the house and no money - you know... well, it looks like some contacts I've made are going to come good - that was the idea after all - to make contacts, so I'll be moving out of here soon and looking a few of them up. Wondered if you'd like to come with me? Back into the musical world – but properly this time?"

She didn't say anything. He always needed someone to be with. To reflect back to him who he was.

He had to admit it was a pretty overwhelming offer and he had to allow her to appear not too enthusiastic.

"You look gorgeous like that." He leaned forward to kiss her bare shoulder but she turned to look at him and he thought better of it. He stood up.

"Alright, alright, I'm sorry. I shouldn't have... But I am sorry Anna. What do you want me to say? I'm apologising to you. I want us to get back together... how can I put it?"

"Allan?" She was putting the top back on the nail-varnish bottle. She looked at him, up and down. "Allan, I think you were a phase I went through - like acne. It makes me blush to think of it. Pathetic. But I'm over it now. Go where you like now, it's got nothing to do with me. Goodbye."

If she had said it with anger, it would have been easier to take than this matter-of-fact indifference.

He stood for a while, wondering if she was putting this on, half-knowing full well that she wasn't.

"Are you going or aren't you?" Her voice was precisely room temperature. She finished her drink.

Allan went back into the kitchen.

Ralph was tasting the bubbling concoction he had cooked and tried to see Allan's expression, surreptitiously, so he could make a guess at the situation. He nearly spilt some of the sauce and put a crick in his neck but Allan's face was blank.

He tried an oblique enquiry.

"Staying for lunch?" he asked. "There's plenty."

"Er, no, I won't be," Allan seemed worn out. "I'll have to go now. Did you put that ring back?"

"Yes, bit too traceable that one. Thanks mate."

Allan picked up his case, "This is the address I'm going to."

"Thanks mate, sure you won't stay and eat?"

"No I... Ralph... do you think I'm pathetic?"

Ralph laughed. "Don't be daft. Why? You'll feel better tomorrow, you see. You always come out on top."

Allan smiled at that. It was true. They shook hands and Ralph saw him to the door. Allan went out and down the steps.

Poor sod.

Pathetic really.

Anna was standing in the bathroom door still wrapped in the towel. "Has he gone?"

"Yes. And whatever it was you said to him, please don't ever say it to me. Where are you going?"

She was halfway across the kitchen and looked back. "Bed. You coming?"

"I haven't finished the pudding yet." She looked at him in disgust.

"Look, I don't do the water-nymph number very often - the least you could do is show some appreciation."

"Oh alright, if you don't mind tinned custard that's fine with me..."

The room they entered was soft luxury: thick carpet under bare feet and soft lights.

"Nice pad innit?"

She went over and kissed him gently on the mouth. After a time, their hands wanted in on the act, exploring faces, running through soft hair and over skin.

They awoke late the following morning, warm together under the duvet. Dinner dishes, empty bottles, clothes and glasses littered every surface. They weren't in any hurry to rush and get breakfast.

Eventually they wandered through and took advantage of the fact that sunken baths have room for two. They could have stayed there for - well, for quite some time, but they had to leave before the owner returned.

The bathroom was full of warm mist, the kitchen was scattered with dishes and pans, a poltergeist seemed to have been dancing in the bedroom and practicing safe sex all over the place.

"I think we've made an impression, shall we go?"

Anna got back her own clothes, with a few small additions. Ralph dug out a year's supply of new threads from the collection he'd found. They took any loose cash they found lying around, figuring that it wouldn't be missed.

They pulled the door closed behind them and faced the street together.

"Our house will be getting flattened soon. Shall we go and watch?"

When they arrived at Wild Rose Court, Reny, Mike and a few others were standing or sitting watching the bailiffs, who had arrived with a police escort just in case, milling about outside their house with orange wire and little warning signs.

The house was now officially empty and sat, quite forlorn, under all this attention. Its wild rhododendron still flourished flamboyantly, innocent of the too many faults that made the house too risky an investment for people who would never see it.

Orange string and navy blue shapes cordoned off the area around both houses to be 'protected' - until the 'dozer arrived. Police stamped and flapped their arms and looked longingly at the scruffy 'trouble' at the end of the street, just out of reach.

"They trying to take off?" said Reny.

"They'll fly one day for sure," said Mike.

He was careful not to put his arm round Reny while they sat there, as that would give the police the excuse to arrest them both for 'obscenity'. Neither of them was yet 21 years old - so could be made a Schedule One offender for having sex with a minor or for 'obscenity'.

"Were you here last night?" Ralph asked. Mike shook his head.

"Sneaked into my house - my parents' - to get some food and stayed. Didn't get out in time this morning though. But nothing happened. I think they might be ready to forgive me - for being me. I think they've realised I'm not a monster from Hell in league with the devil. Mind you, they're not so sure about Reny here..."

"So... great. All we have to do is watch this place getting it and then we can all put up at your mam's?"

"That might be stretching it a bit."

The quiet suburban stillness was pushed away suddenly by a boiling lava of sound coming closer.

The sound turned the corner, bringing a mountain of metal, carrying it slowly and untroubled towards them. The transporter was parked at the top of the street. Everyone kept well out of its way. The 'dozer climbed off its carrier - a king off his howdah - and turned into the street. Jim climbed down from the transporter's passenger seat to watch.

"He didn't waste much time finding another 'dozer!" said Mike. "I thought he was on our side!"

They glared at him in disgust. Jim waved and nodded at them and seemed highly pleased with himself but didn't come over to explain.

"What do you mean," asked Ralph, "another dozer'?"

"I'll tell you later," Reny said, too depressed to talk about it now. They had risked an awful lot for no purpose.

The dozer moved on down the little street - ridiculously slowly for the noise it was making- it sounded like about ten Formula-ones revving up for a race - but massively unstoppable. Some of the respectable residents came out of their houses to watch. The police moved out of the way efficiently and stood in line, dwarfed by the monster moving past them. The driver maneuvered the beast into position.

Swaying very slightly in the early morning sun - grey and rounded, cubical and huge - the demolition-ball hung on the thick black chain carried high on the upraised arm of the yellow tank - as if it had found something disgusting in its lair and was now removing it at arm's-length. If it had had another arm it would have been holding its nose.

It gradually crept to a halt, coughing and shifting, pale delicate clouds of lung-choking, slow poison retching from its back-end and wafting over the street.

Then it stopped.

The police seemed confused and moved away again, looking to each other for reassurance. The world was suddenly quiet. The smoke no longer trailed but hung around the beast and curled upwards, like it was lying there, panting in the cold air, deciding what to do next.

They could see the grey silhouette of the man inside, shifting his gears before releasing it to the hunt. He pulled a lever.

"It's started. Goodbye House!"

The whole, squat rectangular body of the thing swung horribly slowly round on its axis towards 'their' house. The thick metal tracks gripped the earth like claws and the arm carried the massive block towards where Anna and Matt, and Allan for a short time, and Ralph and Suzy and many other had lived, at least for a while. It was as if it was measuring the distance before taking a real swipe, as golfers usually do. The house sat and looked vulnerable, waiting for the end.

"Not even a blindfold."

"He's too far away, he's gonna miss."

The ball had stopped and hung a good ten feet away from what had been Ralph and Anna's kitchen window as if it was peering through the gaps in the boards.

Then slow-motion switched to high speed.

The yellow creature, crouching in the street coughed, revved and roared alive, seeming to flex itself for battle. The pitch of the engine rose higher and louder - but nothing moved.

Then, like a high note sung after the lungs have been filled, or like the first wave of orgasm, all energy was released in a rush. Where there had been slow-motion, now time was oiled. They didn't grasp what was happening until it was finished.

The yellow body swung smoothly and the arm was carried through the air, the chain arched against the sky as the reluctant weight held back, didn't want to follow, hung for a second then toppled after the chain, raced to catch up with it. It hurtled past to lead the way forward, its shadow running over the sunlit street into the shadow of the house on the opposite side - Reny's home, and Liz's and the others - and the engine roar was lost, soaked up, in the cracking roar as bricks shattered and shuddered, split and fell and the echo boomed inside the smitten house like a drum.

Dust flew.

Then the great weight hung at peace in the jagged edged space it had made. The engine purred to itself a little, then began to prepare for a new assault.

They were surprised into silence - they knew it had been too soon for Jim to replace the old plans with the new - but they cheered and applauded and saw Jim joining in, laughing.

It was the wrong house.

The silhouette at the controls didn't hear any of this and shifted gears to finish the job. The police took up comfortable stances to while away the overtime.

Jim came over at last and explained events as far as he understood them.

It seemed the contractors had phoned to say that two of their machines had apparently been mysteriously sabotaged and were out of action so they had had to postpone that day's appointment. Time being money, Carol had passed this efficiently onto Jim who had, with great initiative, volunteered to rush the plans to another contractor so as not to lose the day. He had spent the morning on the phone finding a contractor who could do it - a great show of initiative and commitment.

Such dedication to save loss of investment did not go unnoticed by his superiors (it was hardly his fault that the plans he delivered were for the wrong house to be destroyed. It wasn't his signature on the plans.)

The signature was T.H. - a promising young architect who seemed to have been given too much too soon and to have made this ghastly mistake. The drawings were impeccable but, ridiculously, gave a mirror-image of the correct picture leading to the wrong house having been demolished. Catastrophe. There was no point in going ahead with converting the other house. The margins had always been tight. DCL withdrew interest from the little street and went to find more lucrative pastures leaving it to accrue as real estate until more profitable times.

In the next few days, after investigations had been made, Arthur would dictate, surprisingly fluently, the letter of dismissal and hand it to Tom in person. Arthur received his own, similar letter later in the year when the long-threatened heart-attack finally hit DCL and it turned vicious in its fight to survive. At least Arthur's had a handsome payoff and pension attached in some recognition of a lifetime's devotion.

But for now, the once and future residents, and friends, pooled funds for some celebratory supplies from the cake shop. They sat on the kerb and watched the rest of the economically viable house being dissected. First, like a wounded palace with a section taken out to let visitors see, then a doll's house with bits of scruffy furniture asking to be rearranged, then a bombed house with no all-clear sirens, and then a large pile of bricks with bits of cloth and table-legs sticking out under a cloud of pink-dust.

The trucks arrived and bustled about removing the remains and when they had gone there was a flat concrete jigsaw shape where the house had been.

The other house - whose expensively faulty foundations and mysterious plumbing had reduced its potential profit margin to the unworthwhile was left standing, and became quite crowded after that.

The loss did not bring the might of DCL crashing to the earth nor even cracked one of the plaster cornices of its headquarters - but they had won a place to live and would be left in peace for a while.

All the plans for 'developing' the 'up-market' flats had had to be scrapped.

Later in the year, when Carol, and others on the same grade, learned they were due to lose their jobs as part of the 're-structuring', like her, most of her colleagues had nowhere else to go. They wondered if there was any point in trying to do something to stop the losses. Carol had persuaded them it just might be worth organising something.

Well, you could never tell, could you?

The people working in Jim's section, looking likely to be the next to be attacked. They pledged their support for whatever sort of action the secretaries decided on - and life at DCL looked to become rather more interesting in the near future.

Later in the year, with some small victories behind them, they noticed leaflets were being put up around the town advertising the big, national protest march against the big, national cuts. The people at No. 3 all decided to go on that as it seemed other people had had enough too and were organising something. Some from DCL went too - including Jim and his daughter.

There was a sense of change in the air.

Carol had given up wearing a hair slide and became a regular visitor to Wild Rose Court, where she had met Liz. Liz had smiled at her and Carol had started to realise why it was that she had never really fancied Ken - or any other bloke for that matter.

The people living at No. 3 started work on the ground floor and the basement to make them habitable again. They also found an old summer house in the back garden while they were pushing their way through the weeds in the field that had once been a lawn. They patched it up and cleaned it back to a former glory.

One morning, outside fixing the gate, Ralph switched on his radio. It was March 5th 1984. He listened for a moment then ran to tell the others.

"Did you hear that? The miners are out – on strike – all of them - out to stop job cuts!"

"And?"

"And they might win – they could stop the rot! They could stop Thatcher!"

"They won't win on their own – no one can!"

"Well maybe they won't be on their own - maybe others will strike with them – then she wouldn't stand a chance! This could change all our lives! The other unions might organise strikes in their support – marches, demos!"

"Yeah, and maybe me and Reny will go up the picket lines in a mini bus full of gays!"

Reny looked at him, his face serious. "That's a good idea," he said.

He frowned, planning.

"Yeah right," said Mike. "Like that would ever

happen!"

"Anyway, if you fight you might win – if you don't fight – you'll never win – we know that!"

"Yeah, but miners? They're a tiny minority! The strike will be over in a week!"

"There are 30,000 of them!"

"So? That's less than 1% of the working class in this country – it'll be over in a week – they don't stand a chance! Up against the state…"

Their voices carried up into the afternoon sky.

Great rambling trees and bushes grew here now where once pot plants and crippled bonsais, had broken loose, recovered and made room to grow, untwisted. Tangled plants of all heights were here, in remnant shades of autumn. They looked faded now, after a long winter - but the new growth was already showing through and there was a promise of a new blaze of colour, come the Spring.

Afterword

The miners' strike was to last a year and the miners, less than 1% of the working class of the UK, came very close to winning. They held out for a whole year: New laws were introduced to defeat them; benefit sanctions; the right to move around the country - the police were mobilised as never before, in numbers never seen before. None of the other unions took action alongside them.

The fight to support the miners changed many lives forever. Support of food and solidarity poured in from all communities and from across the world. Many people had their whole world view changed forever by the events of that year....

...And minibuses full of LGBT people drove up to the picket lines to support the miners.

The following year the miners led the Gay Pride march, in solidarity.

Today there are still over a million empty homes in Britain while many go homeless.